Catalpa's Curse

The Willoughby Witches

(Book Three)

by

Terri Reid

D1738289

Catalpa's Curse

The Willoughby Witches
(Book Three)

by Terri Reid

The author would like to thank all those who have contributed to the creation of this book: Richard Reid, Sarah Reid, Peggy Hannah, Mickey Claus, Terrie Snyder, and Ruth Ann Mulnix. And especially to the wonderful readers who are starting this whole new adventure with me, thank you all!

Chapter One

Catalpa Willoughby, the eldest of the Willoughby sisters, sat on a large, intricately embroidered pillow in the corner of the sunroom, her legs folded in a Lotus position, her hands resting lightly on her knees with her thumb and index finger lightly touching each other. Her eyes were closed, and her breathing was deep and slow. The mantra she was mouthing was ancient and powerful, as her mind explored the realms of the unknown.

She was drifting in a sea of gray, but she felt no fear. Her body was relaxed and calm, her thoughts were open, and she felt herself falling further and further into the vastness of her mind. She could see a light in the distance, and she moved towards it. Enlightenment, that's what she needed. The light changed the gray to blue, and she could see a shadowy figure in the distance. She watched him approach, but she could not see him clearly. He stopped and gazed at her.

"It has been a long while since we have spoken, little one," he said with kindness.

"I'm sorry," her mind replied. "I have been busy and have not had time for meditation and reflection."

"You mean you have not taken time," he gently chastised. "Although, you of all people realize how important this is to your energy."

She nodded. "I neglected it, and now I feel the loss."

He paused for a moment, studying her. "And you feel more than loss, you feel pain," he said softly. "Your heart has been changed."

She felt tears springing beneath her closed eyelids, and she nodded. "This has been a painful, yet also joyful, time for our family."

"The joy you feel is for others," he replied. "And the pain, that is your pain to bear."

She sighed. "I am strong," she said. "I can handle a little disappointment."

"This path you are now taking will bring more than a little disappointment," he counseled. "You need not bear the burden by yourself."

"Do you speak of the sorrow in my life?" she asked.

He was silent for a moment. "There is sorrow, yes," he replied. "But I also see a darker path. There will be death."

She immediately thought of Donovan and, like a magician, suddenly his image was before her too.

"You worry about this one," the shadow man said.

She shrugged in her mind, and the action was also copied by her body. "He is one I loved once," she replied, trying to be casual. "Of course, I worry a little."

She could hear the soft laughter and the disbelief. "You are safe here in your journey, little one," he said. "You do not need to lie."

"I do not lie," she replied forcefully.

He was silent for a long moment. "Ah, so now I see," he finally said. "You lie to yourself, not me."

She shook her head. "I do not lie," she insisted.

"You must be wary, little one," the shadow said. "If you do not understand your own heart and your own mind, they can be used as weapons against you."

"He does not love me," she said harshly.

"Just because love is not reciprocated does not mean it does not exist," he replied gently. "Although, one-sided love is a burden to carry rather than wings to lift."

"What kind of person am I who loves where there is no hope?" she whispered. "Who believes when there can be no trust?"

"You have a generous and tender heart, Catalpa," he said. "And although you try to deny it, it is your strongest weapon and your greatest weakness."

"It is my curse," she whispered. "To love and not be loved."

He shook his head. "Perhaps," he agreed. "Or perhaps you have yet to find the courage to use your strongest weapon in your journey."

"What do you mean?" she asked. "How should I use it?"

"That, my little one, is a decision that only you can make," he replied, and then he faded into the blue-gray shadows around her.

Chapter Two

Police Chief Joseph Norwalk stood at the curb, outside of the station, watching the black Suburban move slowly down the street. He had always been a suspicious person, it came with being in law enforcement, but after the experiences that had transpired in the last few months with the Willoughby family, he was even more guarded. A dark car, one that he'd never seen before, sent him into full alert.

He watched the Suburban slow and pull into the parking lot of a Bed and Breakfast on the corner of Center Street and Fremont. He rolled back slightly on his heels; it was probably about time he visited the B&B to ask them about their updated security procedures, he decided. He turned toward his cruiser and stopped.

"Damn," he muttered as Donovan Farrington came walking towards him.

"What's up?" Donovan asked, peering down the road towards the B&B.

"Nothing," Joseph replied immediately, leaning casually against a light pole. "What's up with you?"

Donovan studied Joseph for a moment and shook his head. "I watched you looking down the street," he accused. "You were staring at something."

Joseph shrugged. "Police business," he replied easily, pushing himself away from the pole and moving around Donovan.

Reaching out, Donovan grabbed Joseph's arm to stop him. "You will answer me," Donovan growled, his eyes blazing with power.

Joseph stared back, his amber eyes glowing with equal power. "You forget that I'm not one of your stooges, Donovan," he warned. "That's not a good thing to forget."

"You forget who you are dealing with now," Donovan replied. "With the power…"

"The Master's power?" Joseph interrupted. "Who's controlling who, Donovan?"

Like he was scalded, Donovan released Joseph's arm and stumbled back, shaking his head. "I'm sorry," he said, shaking his head to clear it. "I shouldn't have…"

"You shouldn't have made a deal with the Master," Joseph said.

"I can control it," Donovan said, his voice lowered. "I'm fine. I'm just not used to it."

"It's already been three weeks since the ceremony," Joseph whispered urgently. "And I can already see the change in you. You've got to break the connection."

"I can't," Donovan said. "It's the only way to save Cat."

Joseph shook his head. "No, that's not true, and you know it," he said. "He's using you and your connection to the Willoughbys to defeat them. You're his best weapon."

"The hell I am," Donovan replied harshly. "I'm doing this for them."

Joseph laughed mirthlessly and shook his head.

"And that's just what he wants you to believe," he said. "In the meantime, stay out of my police investigations because I don't trust you."

He started to walk away when Donovan grabbed his arm again.

"I'm on your side," Donovan insisted.

Joseph stared down at Donovan's hand and then looked up into his eyes.

"Then cut the connection," Joseph insisted.

Donovan shook his head, his eyes pleading for understanding.

"You don't understand," Donovan replied. "It's not that simple."

"No, see, you don't understand," Joseph said, turning and facing him. "You think you can control a being who is ancient and powerful. Who knows every trick in the book. Hell, he probably wrote the book. He is using you, just liked he used Bates. And as soon as he was done with Bates, he killed him. Why do you think he'd be any different with you?"

"Because I'm not Bates," Donovan insisted. "I'm special. I have more power than Bates ever had. The Master sees so much potential…"

Joseph grabbed Donovan's upper arms and shook him. "Do you hear what you're saying?" he exclaimed. "He's already in your head. He's already playing you."

Donovan ripped himself out of Joseph's grip and stepped back. "No," he said, shaking his head in confusion. "No. He's not. I'm fine. I'm helping."

Joseph sighed softly. "I think you're a good man, Donovan," he said. "I think you started with pure intentions. But I think you are way in over your head. If you need help to get out, I'll be there for you, man. I promise."

"I can handle this," Donovan replied fiercely. "I don't need your help." He turned and stormed down the street while Joseph watched him.

"Damn it," Joseph whispered. "Be careful, man."

Chapter Three

"Incoming!" Hazel Willoughby screamed as she rushed through the back door, across the kitchen to the powder room. She darted inside and slammed the door behind her.

Agnes Willoughby, Hazel's mother, sighed, shook her head fondly, and went back to chopping the herbs on her counter. "I remember those days," she said.

Rowan picked up the chopped herbs and laid them carefully in dehydrator trays. "Fondly?" she asked.

"No," Agnes said. "Morning sickness is not something anyone enjoys or remembers fondly."

The toilet flushed, and Hazel staggered out of the bathroom, sliding into a chair next to the kitchen table and laid her head on her folded arms. "I think I'm dying," she moaned.

"What was it this time?" Rowan asked, walking across the room to sit down next to her sister.

"The grain for the goats," Hazel groaned. "I always loved that smell, but this morning..." She placed her hand over her mouth and moaned.

Poor baby," Rowan said sympathetically. "How about some tea?"

Her face still buried in her arms, Hazel shook her head. "I'll just projectile vomit it across the room."

"Well, that's a pretty mental picture," Catalpa said as she entered the kitchen from the great room.

Hazel lifted her head slightly and glared at her older sister. "Don't mock the pregnant sister," she said. "Someday this could be you."

Catalpa felt the swift piercing of her heart but didn't let the pain of the remark show on her face. "You're right," she said quickly. "I'm sorry."

Immediately contrite, Hazel stood up and walked over to Catalpa. "No, I'm sorry," she said. "Please don't be sad."

Catalpa took a deep breath and smiled again, but the smile didn't reach her eyes. "I'm okay," she shrugged. "I'm just still learning how to deal, okay?"

Hazel put her arms around her sister and hugged her. "Okay," she said. "Take your time dealing. We're all here for you."

Cat smiled and placed a kiss on her sister's forehead. "Thank you," she replied. "And I highly recommend Rowan's tea; it will make you feel better immediately."

Hazel looked over her shoulder at Rowan. "Immediately?" she asked.

Rowan nodded and grinned. "It's practically magic," she teased.

Hazel sighed. "I hope so," she said. "I really need to concentrate on something other than puking."

Catalpa walked Hazel back to the table, while Rowan stood up and filled the teapot with water. Agnes studied Catalpa, and her heart broke for her eldest daughter. Loving Donovan and losing him years ago had

14

been hard enough, but finding him again and believing him, only to lose him once more, had been even harder.

"You know, he could be telling the truth," Agnes finally said. "He could be on our side."

Cat looked over at her mother and nodded. "He could be," she said. "But we really can't afford to trust him, can we? Especially now that he's accepted the…"

"Mosquito," Hazel inserted. "Remember, we don't want to draw him towards us by using his name."

Cat nodded. "Especially now that he's the mosquito's right-hand man."

"He said he was doing that only because he could protect us," Agnes reminded her.

"Then he's an idiot," Cat replied. "He can't outmaneuver an ancient demon. I've tried to tell him."

"But he won't listen because he wants to protect you," Agnes said.

"Protect all of us," Cat said. "If we can believe him, he wants to protect all of us because we were the only family he ever had."

"And if we can't believe him," Rowan said.

Cat looked across the room and met her sister's gaze. "If we can't believe him and he is on the other side, then he will use every emotional attachment he has with us," she said candidly. "And I know that I'm the most vulnerable because I really want to believe him."

Chapter Four

The black Suburban pulled into the farthest opening in the lot. After a moment, the door opened, and a tall, black man stepped out of the vehicle. Finias Bailey's dark suit jacket fit tautly over his broad shoulders and muscular arms. The sun glistened off his bald head before he slipped on a black fedora. Then, reaching into the vehicle, he pulled out a leather briefcase and placed it on the driver's seat. Opening it, he examined the identification he was going to be using on this trip. *Ellis Thomas*, he repeated in his mind. *Ellis Thomas.* He placed the fake driver's license and credit cards into his wallet and put his true identification and credit cards into the briefcase. Then he sealed the case, clicking down on the small lock, pulled the briefcase out of the car, and closed the car door.

He walked along the side of the old Victorian Mansion and jogged up the porch steps to enter the home at the front lobby. The innkeeper, Katie Flanders, was waiting at the reception desk to meet him.

"Mr. Thomas, Ellis Thomas?" she asked, slightly awed by his large stature.

"Yes, good afternoon. You have a lovely home," his genteel response calmed her nerves immediately.

"Thank you," she replied with a smile. "We love it. I'm Katie Flanders, the owner." She glanced down at her computer and then back up at him in surprise. "You booked the entire second floor. Is there someone else with you?"

He smiled and shook his head. "No, I just prefer my solitude," he said. "Will that be a problem?"

She shook her head. "No, of course not," she replied, handing him his keys. "Can I help you with your luggage?"

He took the keys and then encompassed her hand in his own. "I would not think of having you carry anything for me," he replied with a gallant nod. "I can see to my things. But if you would be so kind as to show me to my room…"

Lost for a moment in his charm and courtesy, it took the innkeeper a moment to process his request. "Oh! Of course," she replied, slipping her hand out of his and rushing around the desk. "Please, come this way."

She led him to a beautiful oak staircase with leaded cut-glass windows that shone on the highly polished steps. Turning, she smiled again. "It's right up here."

He followed her to the upstairs hall, and she opened the first door. "This is the suite," she said. "It has a bedroom, sitting room, and ensuite bath."

He slowly looked around the well-furnished room and nodded. The décor was circa 1900 and fit the atmosphere of the house. "It's lovely," he replied. "I'm sure I will feel quite at home here."

"Oh, where is your home?" she asked. "You didn't say."

He smiled at her and nodded. "No, I didn't, did I?" Then he turned back to the hallway. "And the other rooms?"

"Oh," she replied, slightly nonplussed. "You have two more bedrooms that share a bath in the hall. One has a small sitting room with a television."

He smiled. "That will be relaxing," he said.

"Would you like me to bring fresh linen up every day to all three rooms?" she asked.

He paused for a moment, considering her question. "May I be completely honest with you?" he asked in a hushed tone.

"Of course," she eagerly replied. "Yes. Of course."

"I am here on a somewhat classified assignment," he said, glancing around to ensure their privacy. "Which is one of the reasons I reserved the entire second floor. The assignment I am completing is quite... how should I put this? Crucial."

"Crucial?" she repeated.

He nodded. "Very crucial," he agreed. "Not only for Whitewater, not only for the state of Wisconsin but, literally for the entire country."

She clapped her hand over her mouth. "Oh, my," she gasped. "Do you work for an agency?"

His smile widened, and he nodded slowly. "I see that you understand reading between the lines," he said with approval. "I can't divulge who I am working for, but some call us an alphabet agency."

Her eyes widened, and she nodded wordlessly.

"Therefore, you will understand that access to my rooms will be somewhat limited," he said. "Especially because of the sensitivity of the paperwork I am carrying."

"Of course," she breathed. "Of course."

"I will be happy to change my linen when needed," he said. "And I will also tidy up after myself." He smiled again, showing a mouthful of pearl-white teeth. "I have learned to be quite particular about not leaving any traces behind."

"Oh, well, that's fine. I'm sure," she said. "I can certainly make sure that you get all the privacy you need."

"That would be very helpful," he said, and then, as if it were an afterthought, he added, "Oh, and if anyone comes asking questions about me, I would appreciate your discretion."

"Could there be danger?" she asked, her voice shaking.

He placed a comforting hand on her shoulder and shook his head. "Oh, I don't anticipate danger," he replied. "But I would truly appreciate knowing if anyone comes around asking questions. In order to anticipate any trouble."

"Yes, we don't want any trouble," she repeated, then she took a deep breath and smiled at him once more. "Well, is there anything else I can do?"

"There is one more thing," he replied. "Do you know anything about a family in the area whose last name is Willoughby?"

Chapter Five

Joseph deliberately parked the cruiser next to the black Suburban in the B&B's parking lot. Strolling around the back of the cruiser, he glanced at the license plate on the SUV and then took a quick photo with his phone, so he could run the plate once he got back into the office.

With that taken care of, he followed the same path Finias had followed about thirty minutes earlier. He took his time walking up to the lobby, observing the landmarks around the old B&B and wondering if this location would be advantageous to a member of the other coven.

He looked down Fremont towards the Municipal Building, Donovan's office was about two blocks away from there. The water tower, that had stories and rumors of its own, was less than a mile away in the other direction. He shook his head; there didn't seem to be anything significant about this location that he could see. He would have to ask Hazel.

24

Just thinking her name immediately brought a smile to his lips. He was heading to the Willoughby house after work, so they could continue their plans for ending the curse. It was less than two months from Samhain, or Halloween as he liked to call it, and they were still not close to finding a solution to the problem.

Added to that, things had been heating up in town. Members of the opposing coven, who had always held their cards close to their chest, were now outwardly performing spells and wreaking havoc throughout the city. His officers now all wore amulets courtesy of the Willoughby witches to protect them from curses and spells. He had to smudge his offices and the jail cells daily with white sage to cleanse any residual negative energy. This is not what he'd signed up for when he became an officer of the law.

Feeling a little testy, as he remembered what the damn coven was putting him through, Joseph marched into the B&B with a little more attitude than he had initially intended. He strode over to the reception desk, put his forearms on the counter, and leaned toward Katie, who was typing on her computer.

"Who's the guy in the black Suburban?" he asked bluntly.

She looked up at him and shook her head. "What?"

He nodded in the direction of her parking lot. "The black Suburban parked out in the lot," he said. "Who owns it?"

She shrugged. "That's privileged information."

"I'm the damn Chief of Police," Joseph snarled. "I'm privileged."

She cocked an eyebrow. "Do you have a warrant?" she asked.

"What the hell, Katie?" he blustered. "Since when do I need a warrant for a simple answer."

She shrugged. "Well, it's all about legal protection," she replied. "If I divulge confidential information and my guests find out, they could sue me. Or, even worse, they could post a bad review."

"Katie," he groaned. "This could be important."

Katie looked up at Joseph and bit her lower lip in consternation. She really hated to do this to him, but Ellis had specifically asked her to keep his information confidential. And if he were really from the FBI or the CIA or the NSA, she could be in a lot more trouble than just making Joseph get a warrant. She shook her head.

"Sorry, Chief," she said. "That's my final answer."

Joseph glared at her and shook his head. He hated the fact that she was well within her rights to request a warrant. He hated the fact that he hadn't considered the legal ramifications of encouraging her to disclose private information. And he really hated the fact that he was going to have to go in front of a judge and try to talk her into giving him a warrant without any viable probable cause except a gut feeling.

"I'll remember this, Katie," he said, sliding his forearms off the counter and stepping back.

She stood up and faced him. "And what is that supposed to mean?" she asked.

"Next Fraternal Order of Police Officers Pancake Breakfast," he said with a sneer. "You're not getting a discount."

He turned and walked out, pleased with the surprised chuckle he heard behind him.

"I guess it's time to sweet talk a judge," he said, as he stepped off the front porch.

"Or you could just ask the owner of the vehicle."

Chapter Six

Joseph turned around and looked at Finias, concealing his surprise that the man was as tall as he was. "I guess I could ask the owner," Joseph acknowledged. "Would you happen to be the owner?"

Finias nodded. "I am," he said. "Is there a law in this town against driving black Suburbans?"

Joseph studied the man before him. The man was certainly over forty years of age, but Joseph couldn't be sure how much older. He was well-built and in shape, a shape that Joseph knew you didn't get from the inside of a gym. His eyes were piercing—electric blue—and held Joseph's gaze with calm certainty.

"No, I don't suppose there is," Joseph finally replied. "Unless, of course, the driver is looking to cause some kind of mischief."

A wide smile broke out on Finias' face, and he nodded. "Yes, I could see how that would be a concern," he replied. "However, I am not looking to cause any kind of mischief."

"Do you mind if I ask you why you're in town?" Joseph asked.

The smile remained. "Not if you don't mind me not answering," he replied calmly.

"Actually, I do mind," Joseph replied. "I've got too many things going on in this town to play games with you."

Finias' smile vanished. "Have things already begun?" he asked.

"Which side are you on?" Joseph asked.

Finias lowered his voice. "Do you mean, am I a good witch or a bad witch?" he asked sarcastically.

"No, I'm asking you what the hell you're doing in Whitewater," Joseph snapped. "And if I don't get a good answer, I'm going to throw your ass in jail."

"On what grounds?" Finias asked, folding his arms across his chest.

"Obstruction of justice," Joseph replied, mimicking Finias' stance. "I've got an ongoing investigation here, and I have a feeling you're not telling me everything you know."

"I haven't told you anything at all," Finias declared.

"Exactly my point," Joseph tossed back.

Finias stared at Joseph for a long moment, and then he smiled and nodded. "Okay, I will tell you what I know, on one condition," he replied.

"What?" Joseph asked warily.

"You keep my presence here in Whitewater hidden," Finias replied.

Joseph rolled his eyes. "Yeah, because no one is going to notice a six-foot five black guy with blue eyes in the middle of Wisconsin," he said sarcastically. "Really? Really, you think you can keep your presence a secret."

"You just keep my information confidential and my presence here under wraps," Finias said, "And I'll worry about the rest of the town."

"Before I agree to anything with you, I have one question you have to answer," Joseph demanded.

Finias nodded slowly. "And if I answer, do I have your word that you will keep my presence confidential?"

Joseph nodded.

"Fine, go ahead and ask," Finias said.

"Are you any danger to the Willoughbys?" Joseph asked.

Finias stared straight into Joseph's eyes and shook his head. "No, I do not pose a threat to that family."

"If you are lying to me…" Joseph began.

Finias straightened himself proudly. "I do not lie."

"I heard that before," Joseph replied. "But for now, I'll take you at your word."

"Our agreement, for confidentiality," Finias said. "That includes the Willoughbys. I do not want her…I mean, them to know I am here."

"I gave my word," Joseph said. "And I'll keep it. As long as you keep up your side of the bargain."

"Where do you want to meet?" Finias asked. "I would prefer to meet in the evening."

"Okay, ten-thirty," Joseph said. "Private or public?"

"Private," Finias replied.

Joseph pulled out a card, jotted an address on the back and handed it to Finias. "My apartment," he said. "I'll see you at ten-thirty." He started to turn when Finias reached out and grabbed his arm.

"Aren't you afraid to meet me alone?" Finias asked.

Joseph turned back and smiled, suddenly his eyes glowed with feral light, and his canine teeth sharpened. Then, just as quickly, he was back to his normal self. "Yeah, I don't think so," he said. "I'll see you tonight."

Chapter Seven

Cat slipped the paper booties on over her shoes and put a white lab coat on over her t-shirt and jeans. Her black, curly hair was already wrapped in a colorful scarf, so she decided to opt out of putting the hair net over her head. She turned and looked across the wide expanse from the front door of the production center for their herb distillations and remedies to Rowan's office in the back. She could see Rowan and Henry through the large window and grinned. From the looks of things, they had both forgotten about their meeting.

Pulling her phone from her pocket, she quickly texted her sister. "Get a room."

She watched, delighted, as Rowan pulled away from her embrace with Henry, glanced down at her phone and then looked out through the window. A tinge of pink lit upon Rowan's cheeks, and she laughed, then looked down at her phone and texted back. "I have an entire building; I don't need a room."

Laughing, Cat replied. "Do you want me to come back later?" She added a smoochie-faced emoji and sent it.

Rowan opened the door to the office and called, "No, you've already ruined the moment," she teased. "You might as well come in."

Henry, Cat noted as she entered the large office area, was also wearing a slight tinge on his cheeks and cleared his throat several times before he could speak. "Um, good afternoon, Cat," he managed, his English accent sounding even more proper than usual.

"It's still morning, Henry," Cat replied, biting back a smile.

He glanced down at his watch, ran his hand through his hair, making it even more ruffled than Rowan's hands had done, and sighed. "So, it is," he said, shaking his head. "So it is."

Cat pulled a tissue from a box and handed it to him before sitting down at the meeting table. "Lipstick," she said, not bothering to hide her grin this time. "On your lips. The shade doesn't suit you at all."

Rowan hid her smile behind her hand as she sat down next to her sister. "It really wasn't that noticeable," she assured him.

Henry rubbed his lips hurriedly, disposed of the tissue, and took his seat at the table. "I have totally lost any shred of dignity," he said.

"Well, when it's lost for love," Cat replied, "it's understandable."

Her heart tightened when she saw the two lovers clasp hands without thought as they pulled their notes in front of them.

"Okay," Henry said, his voice now business-like, as he looked down at his information. "I've reviewed the text from the part of the grimoire we were allowed to read."

"Wait? What?" Cat asked.

Henry looked up at Cat. "The grimoire we were given, the one Patience hid away, is only partially opened," he explained. "There is a spell on it that won't allow us to read further at this time."

"Why not?" Cat asked.

Rowan shook her head. "You're not going to like the answer," she said.

"Try me," Cat replied.

"Our ancestors were pretty specific about what we needed in order to fight the demon," Rowan said, then she looked down at her papers and read. "The three must find partners, those of the blood, who love deeply enough to sacrifice themselves for the quest. Without the three (and, perhaps, one more soul) the beast will not be conquered, and humanity will be defeated."

She looked up and met her sister's eyes. "Then at the end of their message, they said, 'We ask you now, our dear family, to find those partners and then return to this grimoire within the safety of a circle to read more of your task.'"

"So, we can't learn any more until I find a match," Cat said softly.

Rowan nodded. "Yes," she replied. "I'm so sorry."

Shaking her head, Cat looked away from Henry and Rowan and stared out the window. "I can't trust Donovan," she whispered sadly. "I don't know whose side he's on."

"But can you love anyone else?" Henry asked quietly.

Cat shrugged. "I don't know," she replied, laughing mirthlessly. "I've never tried."

"And just where are we going to find an acceptable partner who's of the blood in Whitewater?" Rowan asked. "It's not like someone fitting that description drives into town every day."

Chapter Eight

Donovan slammed his office door behind him and stormed over to his desk. "I can handle this," he muttered. "Norwalk has no idea what he's talking about."

He cradled his head in his hands, closed his eyes, and took several measured breaths. He needed to be strong. Not only for himself, but for Cat. For the entire Willoughby family, he owed them that much. Lifting his head, he glanced at the full-length mirror hanging on the small closet in the corner of the room. Putting his hands on the edge of the desk, he pushed himself up and, still watching himself in the mirror, slowly walked over to stand in front of it

Standing a less than a foot away from the mirror, he opened his suit jacket. Then he loosened his tie and slipped it over his head and placed it on the chair behind him. Reaching up to the top of his shirt, he slowly unbuttoned it, pulling the shirttails out of his slacks until the shirt lay loosely open. He took a deep breath, grabbed hold of either side of the shirt, and slowly opened it. The five red, oozing welts bisected his abdomen and wrapped around his body. Still watching himself in the mirror, he lightly touched one of the wounds and winced in pain.

"Boot camp," he whispered, staring at the welts. "It's just like boot camp. Break you down to build you up. I can handle it."

He lifted his head, stared into his own eyes, and softly chanted a spell.

"Remove the mask upon my face,

Remove the glamour others see,

Reveal the truth, the spell replaced,

For as I will, so mote it be."

For a moment, the face in the mirror was a blurry oval, but then it became clearer and more distinct. The handsome face that Cat had fallen in love with was now sunken and pale. His dark, piercing eyes were surrounded with dark shadows. His cheekbones more pronounced and his lips, chapped and dry.

"I can do this," he whispered, but there was doubt in his eyes. He took a deep breath. "I have to do this. There is no other way."

Donovan.

The snake-like voice sent a shudder through his body. The voice surrounded him, yet he knew it could not be heard by others.

"Yes, Master," he replied, trying not to let his revulsion temper his words.

"There is a new entity in town," the Master said. "Find it and destroy it."

"But we don't even know who or what it is," he replied. "It could be helpful…"

"Are you questioning me?"

Donovan gasped in pain as another long, jagged cut appeared on his stomach. "No," he breathed. "No, I'm not."

"The last Willoughby bitch needs a mate," the Master snarled. "Anyone who could be a partner to her is an enemy. Destroy him."

"What?" Donovan exclaimed, taken by surprise.

The Master snickered with satisfaction. "That's right, you are attracted to the bitch, aren't you?"

"That was a long time ago," Donovan replied, cursing himself for reacting. "She means nothing to me. She is just an obstacle for us to overcome."

"Good," the Master praised. "And for that, I will let you share some of her blood as she dies. It will be very sweet and will give you even more power."

"Drink her blood?" Donovan asked, confused. "Why would you…"

The evil laughter echoed in his mind. "Fool," the Master taunted. "Blood is the wine of life. Blood is the transporter of power. Blood is the essence of magic."

Donovan shook his head. "You sound like a vampire," he said, trying with all he had to make the tone light and slightly mocking.

The laughter increased to a near hysterical chant. "Do you not understand that all folktales have a seed of truth buried within them?" he asked. "I am not the undead;

I was never born of human flesh, which is why I crave it. Why I long to feast upon it, the sweet blood of those witches will be ambrosia on my lips."

Suddenly Donovan could see in his mind's eye the desires of the Master. He saw the bodies of the Willoughbys laid out on an altar, a sacrifice to evil. He watched in horror as a dark shadow passed over Cat, he heard her screams and then he felt the coppery taste of her blood in his mouth.

He looked up and stared into the mirror, watching a droplet of blood slide from his mouth down his chin. He clapped his hand over his mouth and ran to the waste basket, emptying the contents of his stomach into the receptacle. He heaved into it, over and over again, until he collapsed onto the floor next to his desk.

"Don't worry my boy," the Master whispered into his mind. "It's an acquired taste. And once you acquire it, you will thirst for it for the rest of your life."

Chapter Nine

Hazel sipped on a tall glass of iced herbal tea and sighed with relief. "Four hours," she said triumphantly to her mother sitting on the deck next to her.

Her mother looked up from her tablet and turned to her daughter. "Four hours of what, dear?" she asked.

"Four hours without throwing up," Hazel replied, lifting her glass in the air in a mock toast. "Rowan is a genius. I think she cured my morning sickness."

Agnes looked down at her tablet and then up at Hazel and shook her head. "No, she didn't," she said.

Confused, Hazel shook her head. "What? Yes, she did."

"No, she didn't," Agnes said. "It's four o'clock in the afternoon. You couldn't have morning sickness now if you wanted. You would have afternoon sickness."

Hazel rolled her eyes. "Oh, you are such a comedienne, mom," she began, then her eyes widened, and a look of shock came into her eyes. "Did you say it was four o'clock?"

She placed her cup down and sprang out of her chair.

"Yes, dear. Why?" Agnes asked.

"Because Joseph will be here any moment," Hazel exclaimed, she cupped her hand over her mouth and blew into it. Then she screwed up her face. "And my breath smells like throw-up!"

Agnes bit back a smile and nodded in what she hoped was a solicitous way. "Take some of the mint leaves growing in the pot in the kitchen," she suggested. "That will get rid of bad breath."

"And put green stuff in my teeth," Hazel countered, hurrying towards the door. "No, I'm just going to run upstairs and brush my teeth ten times and then gargle afterwards."

"Good plan," Agnes said. "And I'll just keep Joseph company in the meantime."

Hazel froze and turned to her mother. "You're not going to show him any old photos albums, are you?"

Agnes openly grinned this time. "Time's a wasting, dear," she said.

Grumbling, Hazel hurried through the doorway and rushed toward the staircase.

"What's the problem?" Cat asked, walking in from the living room.

Hazel turned and stopped in her tracks once again. Cat looked amazing. Her curly hair was loose and flowing over her shoulders. She was dressed in a copper-colored, form-fitting dress that made her caramel-colored skin glow. Her gold necklace and earrings glimmered with warmth, and her matching copper-colored heels added three inches to her already tall frame.

"You look amazing," Hazel said. "Where are you going?"

Cat shrugged. "Just out," she said.

Hazel studied her sister for a long moment. "Wait, you're dressed like that, and you think you are going out by yourself?" she said, shaking her head. "Yeah, I don't think so."

"Remember, you're the little sister," Cat said. "You don't get to tell me what to do."

"Doesn't matter," Hazel replied. "With all that's going on, you're stupid to think any of us would let you go somewhere alone." Then her jaw dropped. "You weren't going to let us know. You were going to sneak out!"

Ticked off at being caught, Cat shook her head. "I'm thirty years old," she replied. "I don't have to ask anyone's permission to go out."

The kitchen door opened behind them and closed with a snap. "Oh, I'm afraid you do," Agnes said firmly.

"Mom," Cat said. "I'm going out. And that's it."

"Fine," Hazel said. "I'm going with you."

Cat shook her head. "You can't," she argued. "You spend the entire day puking your guts out."

"I'm cured," Hazel countered and then she closed her eyes for a moment. When she opened them, she was dressed in a short red dress and heels.

"Hey, where is…" Joseph asked as he let himself in the kitchen door, but once he saw Hazel, he stopped dead in his tracks. "Wow, you look amazing!"

She grinned at him. "Thanks," she replied. "We thought we'd go out tonight."

"Works for me," he said, coming up to her. He bent his head down to kiss her, and she slipped her hand over her mouth.

"Hold that thought," she mumbled behind her hand. "And give me another minute."

She closed her eyes again, this time concentrating on a spell that would freshen her breath. When she ran her tongue over her teeth and tasted the minty freshness, she dropped her hand from in front of her mouth, wrapped her arm around his neck, and kissed him with gusto.

When the kiss ended, Joseph leaned back and smiled at her. "Well, that was certainly worth waiting for," he said, his voice deep with desire. "Want to go another round?

Hazel sighed regretfully and shook her head. "I can't because we're fighting."

"What?" Joseph asked, confused. "Why are we fighting?"

"No, we're not fighting," she explained, pointing back and forth between the two of them. "We're fighting." And she pointed to Cat.

Joseph turned and looked over at Cat. "Wow, Cat, you look great," he said. "Where are you going?"

"Out," Cat replied.

"Nowhere," Agnes said at the same time.

"With us," Hazel said.

Joseph looked from one woman to the other. "So, this is one of those instances where I should just step back and not say anything, right?" he asked.

"Cat thinks that she's going to go out tonight all by herself," Hazel said to him.

Joseph turned to Hazel and then back to Cat, and suddenly, he was wearing his cop face. "You're a smart woman, Cat," he said, his voice firm. "You've seen what's happened in the past few months to the other members of your family. What in the hell are you thinking?"

Cat sighed, placed one hand on her hip, and stared back at him. "The grimoire said that each of us needs a partner for the rest of the spell to be revealed," she said angrily. "Unless you can conjure a man out of thin air, I need to find someone. He needs to be of the blood, he needs to be brave, and he needs to love me. We're running out of time. So, I have to go out."

Joseph thought back to the man he'd met on the street that afternoon. He was certainly of the blood, he looked like someone women would be attracted to, and he took him on, so he had to be brave. Joseph shrugged. Or stupid.

"I think I've got someone for you," he said.

"What?" Cat asked, astonished. "Where…"

"I can't answer any questions right now," Joseph said. "But I'm meeting with him later tonight. I'll set up a meeting, so you can get to know him and see what you think."

"Do you trust him?" Cat asked.

"Yeah, but I want to check him out a little more before I let you meet him," he said. "Is that okay with you?"

Sighing, Cat kicked off her heels and nodded. "That's great with me," she said. "I hate going out. Almost as much as I hate wearing high heels."

Joseph nodded. "But you looked great," he said, then he turned to Hazel. "Does that mean you're going to change too?" He eyed the short, tight red dress hopefully.

She stepped up and put her hands against his chest. "I suddenly feel like going dancing," she said softly, placing a kiss on his lips. "And there's this quiet little place I know about."

"Sounds perfect," he replied. "Do I know it?"

She grinned. "Oh, yes, you are very well acquainted with it."

She turned to her mom. "We'll be in the barn if anyone needs us," she said and then she led Joseph out of the room.

Cat sighed. "They are so perfect together," she said enviously.

Agnes turned to Cat. "You'll find someone you can give your heart to," she said, giving Cat a quick hug and then going back out to the deck.

Cat watched her mother walk away and nodded, brushing away an errant tear. "The problem is getting it back from the one who already has it," she whispered to herself.

Chapter Ten

Joseph pulled up in front of his apartment at 10:20 and wasn't surprised to see Finias leaning up against his black Suburban that was parked across the street. Joseph got out of his car, looked across the street at Finias, turned, and walked over to his apartment. Finias met his eyes for a brief second, nodded negligibly, pushed himself away from his SUV, and casually crossed the street.

Joseph waited for Finias inside the front lobby of the apartment building. Once he heard the door close behind him, he glanced over his shoulder and nodded. "Okay, the gang's all here," Joseph said, opening the inner door and leading him up the stairs.

He unlocked his apartment door and invited Finias inside. "You're not like a vampire, right?" Joseph asked as Finias walked past him. "Where you have to be invited in?"

Finias smiled and looked back over his shoulder to Joseph. "It's a little late to ask me that question now, isn't it?"

Joseph shrugged. "I watched Van Helsing," he replied. "Werewolf versus vampire. Werewolf wins, hands down."

Finias laughed, a rich, full-bodied sound. "I have seen that movie too," he replied. "And I agree, hands down. Good thing I am not a vampire."

Joseph closed the door and locked it, then turned to Finias. "So, what are you?" he asked.

"I'm a witch," Finias replied. "Actually, I'm an Obeah-man, my bloodline traces back for centuries."

"I thought I heard a little of the islands in your speech," Joseph said. "Where are you from?"

"Jamaica is my home," Finias replied.

"Jamaica and Obeah?" Joseph repeated. "Isn't that practice illegal now?"

"As was witchcraft in your country in its early days," Finias explained. "Those who do not understand, often fear. And fear leads to a desire to control."

Joseph thought about the Willoughby witches and smiled. "Yeah, good luck with that," he said.

He motioned for Finias to take a seat at the table and then walked over to the refrigerator in the tiny kitchen. "Get you something to drink?" he asked.

"Water would be good," Finias replied.

Joseph grabbed two bottles of water, brought them over to the table, handed one to Finias, and then sat down across from him. "So, laws against witches are created by people who fear their power."

"Exactly," Finias agreed. "Rather than try to understand, they forbid. Which only made us go underground and use our abilities in secret. But we are still a strong and powerful force in defending our country."

"How about defending our world?" Joseph asked.

"I have heard about the legend here," Finias said. "And I have felt a shift in the power around us. The dark is becoming stronger."

"What have you heard about the legend?"

"Your country has a sad history of trying to destroy the things it fears, rather than trying to understand them," he said. "The witches who went underground during the Salem Trials ended up moving west to this area of Wisconsin more than one hundred years ago."

Joseph took a sip of his water and nodded.

"At the same time, an institute of spiritualism also came to the area," Finias continued, then he paused and shook his head. "Do you not find it a great coincidence that all of these events occurred at the same time."

Joseph put his bottle down and shook his head. "I don't believe in coincidences," he said.

Finias sat back in his chair and studied Joseph for a moment. "So, you feel this was pre-destined to happen?" he asked.

"No, I believe that often we allow ourselves to be influenced by what we assume are noble motives," he said. "But later, we discover that we have been played like puppets on a string."

"The Willoughby Witches were puppets?" Finias asked, one eyebrow lifting in doubt.

Joseph shook his head. "If they were anything like the Willoughby women today, they were too smart to be played," he said. "No, their part in this was that they got to clean up the mess."

Finias lifted his bottle in a toast. "And history once again repeats itself," he said.

Joseph lifted his bottle and drank. "Okay, I'm beginning to like you," he said. "Why are you here?"

Finias shrugged. "I don't know yet," he said. "I was summoned."

"By who?" Joseph asked. "The mosquito?"

Finias stared in confusion. "I'm sorry, what did you say?"

Embarrassed, Joseph rolled his eyes. "I apologize," he said. "We have a code name for the entity because saying the title it named itself only gives it more power."

"So, you have called it a blood-sucking, annoying pest," Finias said, nodding with approval. "How very appropriate."

"Back to my question," Joseph said. "Who summoned you?"

"The forces for good," Finias replied. "Whatever you wish to call them. But the forces for good realize that we are at a place in the history of the world where evil could actually displace good. We cannot allow that to happen, because once it does, the world will be destroyed."

"What?" Joseph asked. "What do you mean?"

"The world, Mother Earth, this globe we live on," Finias explained. "It has a soul, just like every one of us. And her soul is pure. Her soul is uplifting. Her soul is noble. If the forces of evil become too strong, her soul will shatter. We will witness the destruction of the earth, as was foretold by prophets in the past. When there is too much evil in this world, the spirit of the earth is wounded and reacts."

"Vengeance is mine, saith the Lord," Joseph replied.

"Ah, but vengeance is not revenge," Finias explained. "Vengeance is the consequence of not obeying the laws of truth. When we allow evil to flourish, we must accept the consequences for those actions."

Joseph sat silently for a few long moments, sipping his water and studying the man seated across from him. The guy was real. All of his years as a cop told him, this guy was genuine and was on their side. His mind made up, Joseph put his water bottle down and sat back in his chair. "Okay, I have one more question for you," he said.

Finias nodded. "Go on."

"Are you single?"

Chapter Eleven

"I beg your pardon?" Finias asked, his blue eyes wide with surprise. "What in the world does that have to do with what we're discussing?"

Joseph remained relaxed in his chair and shrugged. "You gonna answer?"

Finias huffed impatiently. "Yes, I am single," he said. He leaned forward on the table and met Joseph's eyes angrily. "Not that it is any of your business, but there has only ever been one woman in my life. We both knew that we couldn't be together for long, so we cherished the time we had. Are you satisfied?"

Joseph nodded. "Yeah, I am," he said easily. "So, do you date?"

"Didn't you just hear me?" Finias exclaimed. "What the hell is this about?"

Joseph sat forward in his chair, his easy-going manner gone. "Let's say there's a special book," he said.

"A grimoire that was written by the sisters who cast the initial spell."

"That would be a vital piece of information," Finias said.

"This grimoire is only allowing the Willoughbys to read a portion until certain conditions are met," Joseph continued.

"Conditions like what?" Finias asked.

"The three from one is not enough," Joseph replied. "Each of the three needs to find a companion, a soul mate, who is of the blood, to help her. Only then will the grimoire reveal the rest of the instructions."

"And the sisters are having problems finding those soulmates?" he asked, his tone skeptical.

"Well, yes and no," Joseph replied with a shrug. "They have each found them, but one of the men thinks he can pretend to be on the side of evil while advocating for the sisters. His name is Donovan Farrington, and he is a powerful warlock."

"He's an idiot," Finias stated bluntly.

Joseph nodded. "Yeah, I agree," he said. "But he's in superhero mode, and he thinks he can save them all by himself."

"Do you trust him?" Finias asked.

Joseph thought about it for several moments, remembering Donovan's remarks when they met on the street that morning. "No. Not anymore," he finally said. "I believe he started on our side. I think he still believes he's doing what's best for the Willoughbys. But I think this creature has far more influence over him than he realizes."

"It will kill him if it believes he is trying to betray it," Finias said.

"Yeah, and Catalpa's heart will die along with him," Joseph said.

Finias sat up a little straighter. "This man is linked to Catalpa?" he asked.

Joseph nodded. "Yeah, why? Do you know her?" he asked suspiciously.

Finias shook his head. "No, we have never met," he answered honestly. "But I have heard of her."

"Okay, so now you know the story," Joseph said. "Now you know why I asked you if you were single. So, now I'm going to ask you one more question."

Finias nodded.

"Do you think you could love Catalpa?" Joseph asked. "Do you think you could be that companion?"

"I do not know if I could be that companion," Finias replied. "Especially if her heart has already been given to this man, Donovan. But I am willing to try."

"Great," Joseph began.

"But there are conditions," Finias added.

"Why do I get the feeling that you're hiding something from me?" Joseph asked.

"Because you're a smart man and I am hiding something," Finias replied. "But it is not something that will harm the Willoughbys. I give you my word of honor."

"What are your conditions?" Joseph asked.

"I meet Catalpa at a neutral place without her family," he replied.

"No," Joseph said. "I don't know you, and you're not going to be alone with her without someone else."

"You don't have much time before Samhain," Finias replied. "And Catalpa will not be able to relax with all of her family watching."

"And she'll be able to relax having dinner with a stranger?" Joseph asked skeptically.

"Are you one of the other companions?" Finias asked.

"Yeah," Joseph said, nodding slowly. "Yeah, I am. Why?"

"Which sister?" Finias asked.

"Hazel, the youngest."

"Fine, you and Hazel can also come," Finias offered. "Tomorrow night?"

"Yeah, tomorrow night," Joseph said. "I can trust you, right?"

Finias sighed and nodded. "I can promise you that harming Catalpa is the furthest thing from my mind."

Joseph started to stand up, then stopped and sat down. "I just realized that I don't know your name," he said. "And you haven't shown me any identification."

Finias smiled and nodded. "You're right," he said. "You don't, and I haven't."

"I'd like to see some now," Joseph asked, holding out his hand.

Finias reached into his back pocket and pulled out a wallet. Reaching inside, he pulled out a Jamaican driver's license and handed it to Joseph.

Joseph took the card, glanced at it, and then met looked up. "You don't mind if I run this through the system to make sure you don't have any outstanding arrest warrants, do you..." Joseph looked back down at the license. "Ellis Thomas."

Finias smiled and shook his head. "I don't mind at all."

Chapter Twelve

The early-morning sun was streaming through the windows in the kitchen of the Willoughby house. A unique fragrance of herbs and floral scent filled the air as Rowan stood at the commercial stove mixing an herbal ointment slowly in a large stainless-steel pot.

Hazel was on her phone at the table, sipping on a cup of the tea Rowan had created for her, and checking her social media accounts. Agnes was sorting through the mail order requests they'd received the day before, and Henry was doing research on his computer.

"Good morning," Joseph said, as he entered the room, then walked over to Hazel and kissed her.

She smiled up at him and returned the kiss. "Good morning," she replied. "Want some tea?"

He shook his head and pulled up a chair next to her. "I'm good," he said. "Where's Cat?"

"She's in her office," Agnes said. "Going through the online orders, while I go through the old-fashioned print orders."

"People still mail in orders?" he asked, astonished.

Agnes nodded. "Some of our older customers have been shopping with us for decades, and they see no reason to change their ways," she said. "So, we accommodate both ends of the technical spectrum."

"Besides," Cat said with a smile as she entered the kitchen from the great room. "Mom is pretty much of that generation."

"Rude," Agnes said. "I'm not that much older than you. And once you turn forty, we'll practically be the same age."

Cat sighed as she walked over to the refrigerator. "Unfortunately, that's true," she said, pulling out a pitcher of cucumber water and pouring herself a glass. "I'll be forty, and you'll be sixty, and we will be the same age."

"Well, that's not for ten years," Agnes said. "And thinking about it only depresses me. So, let's talk about something happier."

"How about the world possibly ending on Samhain?" Hazel suggested. "Then neither of you have to worry about aging."

"Wow, Debbie Downer," Cat said, taking a sip of the water. "Besides, the world is not going to end. We are going to prevail."

"Speaking of the world ending," Joseph said. "I got you a date."

All the women in the room turned toward him, with astonishment in their faces. "Excuse me?" Catalpa asked.

"Oh. No," Joseph stammered. "I didn't mean it that way. Oh hell, I really stepped in it, didn't I?"

Hazel snorted and nodded. "Yes, you did," she agreed.

"What I meant is that you needed to find someone who is of the blood and on our side," he added quickly.

"And I found someone that I think could work. If you're interested, he'd like to meet you for dinner tonight."

Cat placed her glass down on the counter, her stomach tied in knots. "I suppose," she said, trying to push past the sadness in her heart. Then she smiled at Joseph. "Yes, thank you, I need to meet someone. I'd be happy to meet him tonight."

"Okay, so it's not weird, Hazel and I will be joining you," Joseph said. "And, if for any reason, you start feeling uncomfortable or just not interested, we'll leave."

"Thank you," Cat said. "That's helpful."

"Maybe we should come up with a code term that you could use if you aren't interested," Hazel suggested.

Cat rolled her eyes. "Okay, how about something like, 'I'm sorry, this just isn't working for me, I'm not interested,'" she suggested.

"Yeah, well, you kind of took all the fun out of the whole code term thing," Hazel teased. "But I think we can work with that."

"What time?" Cat asked.

"How about six?" Joseph asked. "I'll pick you both up."

"How about I follow you in my car," Cat suggested. "Then, if things go well, we have our options open?"

"Catalpa," Agnes inserted. "Maybe you should go with…"

"Mom," Cat interrupted. "I promise I won't do anything foolish. But I just feel like I need to open myself up to new possibilities."

"But you'll be careful?" Agnes requested.

Cat walked over and placed a kiss on her mother's head. "Of course," she said. "We all know what's at stake here."

"Okay, this is interesting," Henry said, looking up from his laptop at the kitchen table and surprised there were so many people around him. "Oh, hello Joseph and Cat. When did you arrive?"

"What's interesting?" Rowan laughed as she sprinkled some dried comfrey into the ointment.

"The Pratt Institute was made into a Bed and Breakfast," he said.

Hazel nodded and put her cup down. "Oh, yeah, I knew that," she said. "It's the big one downtown."

"Have you ever been there?" Henry asked.

Rowan shook her head. "No," she replied. "It hasn't been the Institute for over fifty years."

"But there could be residual information still in the building," Henry said.

"Residual information—like ghosts?" Agnes asked. "Why would ghosts be helpful, Henry?"

"Well, if we knew what the people who had conjured up the demon said when they were performing the séance," he mused. "It might be helpful when we're trying to banish him."

"So, we should have a séance to find out what went wrong with another séance?" Hazel asked.

Henry shook his head. "Heaven forbid," he exclaimed. "No, I would never recommend a séance, especially in this highly charged environment. I was thinking along the lines of a spirit box or an EVP session."

"That could be interesting," Cat said. "And I understand that the Bed and Breakfast doesn't use the third floor at all. They've locked it up and just have storage up there."

"Why don't they use it?" Joseph asked.

Agnes smiled knowingly. "Well, you're correct when you assume there might be residual energy there," she said. "There was so much residual energy that the B&B has changed hands several times in the past fifty years. And most of the complaints were from rooms on the third floor."

Chapter Thirteen

Finias entered the dining room at the Bed and Breakfast and smiled at Katie. "Good morning," he said with a cordial smile.

"Mr. Thomas, good morning," Katie greeted him with a warm smile. "And how did you sleep?"

"Like I was sleeping on feathers," he replied. "Until I was awoken by the heavenly scent that must be coming from your kitchen."

Katie blushed with pleasure. "Why, what a nice thing to say," she said. "I've made a spinach and ham quiche, chocolate-filled croissants and a fruit salad. How does that sound?"

"Like I will have to go jogging several times a day to work off my breakfast," he replied. "But it will be worth every step."

She chuckled delightedly and then offered him a chair. "Please, have a seat," she said. "And help yourself to a beverage. I'll be serving breakfast in a minute or two."

Seating himself, he picked up a carafe of tomato juice and filled a small juice cup. He picked up the glass and began to sip when Joseph walked through the lobby into the dining room.

"Should I worry that you're drinking blood?" he asked softly, glancing around to be sure Katie was not in the vicinity.

Finias laughed. "You must realize I am sitting in full sun," he said. "So, your vampire theory is not holding up." Then he smiled at Joseph. "Besides, I do not glitter."

Joseph pulled out a chair and sat at the table. "Okay, here's the deal," he said. "I set up the dinner tonight, with Cat, and she agreed. Hazel and I will be there too." He paused for a moment and met Finias' eyes. "You hurt her, and I will kill you."

Finias picked up the glass of tomato juice, sipped again, and then placed it down in exactly the correct spot in the table setting. He picked up the linen napkin and blotted his lips. "I have already given you my word that I do not intend to hurt Catalpa, and I am on your side," he said slowly.

Joseph sat back in the chair and shrugged. "Yeah, well, I'll believe your word when you've proven that it's true," he said.

"That's fair," Finias replied. "So, where are we meeting for dinner?"

Joseph paused for a moment; then a slight smile curled the edge of his mouth. "A brew pub a couple of blocks away from here," he said. "I think you'll like it. It's called Second Salem. We'll meet at six."

A grin spread across Finias' face, his white teeth a dazzling contrast to his dark skin. He lifted the juice again and toasted in Joseph's direction. "I think I will too," he said. "I will see you there at six."

Joseph stood up and nodded slightly. "See you then," he said, and quietly exited the room.

"Were you speaking with someone?" Katie asked a moment later as she carried in a large plate laden with Finias' breakfast.

"No," Finias replied immediately. "Why do you ask?"

She sighed and put the plate on the table in front of him. "You don't get spooked by paranormal things, do you?" she asked.

He bit back a smile and shook his head. "No, I tend to be quite boring and rational," he replied.

She scooted into the chair next to him and turned to face him. "Please, eat your breakfast, I don't want it to get cold," she insisted.

"I will, as long as you tell me about your house," he agreed.

"Well, there are quite a few stories about this Bed and Breakfast," she said. "People have had experiences here that have frightened them. Ghostly experiences."

Finias pulled off a bit of the croissant and popped it into his mouth. "Downstairs?" he asked.

She shrugged. "Well, not that often," she said. "But I always hear conversations happening when I know that I'm the only one home."

"Old houses do that sometimes," he replied.

She smiled. "Exactly," she agreed. "But there have been things that happened upstairs, on the third floor, that just could not be explained. That's why we closed it off."

"Oh," Finias said, picking a forkful of quiche. "Were they dangerous?"

"Well, I suppose you could say that," she said regretfully. "Furniture moving, doors slamming, water faucets turning on, lights flashing."

The fork stopped before he put the morsel in his mouth. "That is quite extraordinary," he said, feigning alarm. "Is it safe for me to be on the second floor?"

"Oh. Oh, yes," she replied, waving her hands as if to dispel any worries. "The second floor is fine. And the only way to get up to the third floor is a locked door at the far end of your hallway. So, really, you are quite safe."

He took the bite of quiche into his mouth and then smiled at her. "This is quite delicious, Katie," he replied. "The cheese in the quiche is unique, is it local?"

"Funny you should ask that," she replied. "Yes, it is, and I'm going to be running out after breakfast to pick up some more and a few other things I need. I'll lock the front door behind me, but your room keys will also open the front door if you decide to go out."

She paused, thinking about what she'd just told him about the building. "Are you going to be okay staying here by yourself?"

He smiled at her and nodded. "Oh, yes, I can assure you that my work will keep me very busy while you are gone," he replied. "And I am not at all concerned about the third floor."

Chapter Fourteen

Cat hiked up the path that led from the side of their home up into the woods and bluffs. With Fuzzy at her side, she was able to concentrate less on her surroundings and more on the ebb and flow of the energy enveloping her. She breathed deeply and inhaled the scent of the rich, moist earth at her feet. She felt the warmth of the sun against the back of her head. Heard the whisper of the wind through the pine trees. And felt the vibrations from the limestone bluffs around her.

She stepped up, grabbing onto a sapling with one hand, and pulled herself up onto the black escarpment that lay above the lake. Walking along the edge, the wind flowing through her hair, she hurried, surefooted, to a ledge a little wider than the path she was on. Once she'd reached the edge, she turned to the small cave nearly concealed by overgrown brush, and slowly entered it.

The cave was no more than five feet deep and was actually more of a shelter than an actual cave. The floor was clay and rock, and the walls nearly smooth limestone with water stains running down from the top. She walked to the very back of the shelter and placed her hand on a smooth stone embedded in the limestone wall. Closing her eyes, she allowed the energy from the stone to fill her body and the memories of that day long ago, fill her mind.

Thunder rumbled, and lightning flashed on the other side of the lake. There was no way she would make it home without getting drenched. Besides, her mother had always warned her not to run through the forest during a lightning storm. She was on the escarpment, and the soft rain had begun to make it slick and dangerous. She hugged the edge of the bluff and moved along its face, hoping to find a place where she could shelter until the storm passed.

She closed her eyes for a moment and reached out to the universe for direction. The answer came almost immediately and clearer than any she'd ever received. Only a few more feet and there would be a shelter. She would be safer there.

Hurrying, trying to avoid getting her hair even wetter, she dashed forward, the memory of the vision guiding her way. The rain increased and she sprinted ahead, laughing with delight as the raindrops splashed against her skin. She dashed into the shelter and then screamed with surprise as she careened into the young man who had also sought shelter from the storm.

He wrapped his arms around her, so she didn't slip on the slick surface and held her in his arms for a long moment. She looked up into his dark, brown eyes, and her heart skipped a beat. Embarrassed, and a little fearful, she slowly stepped away from his embrace.

"I'm so sorry," she apologized. "I had no idea this shelter was taken. I'll go..."

She started to turn, but he placed his hand on her rain-soaked arm. "Stay," he pleaded. "I'll leave if you're uncomfortable. But I want you to stay."

A flash of lightning illuminated the inside of the shelter, and Cat jumped closer to him. She looked over her shoulder at the storm and then back into his face. "I suppose that answers that," she said with a shy smile. "I

think we are both staying."

A reluctant smile grew on his face. "I guess we

are," he agreed.

"I'm Cat..."

"I know who you are," he interrupted.

Her smile vanished immediately, and she sighed.

"Oh," she said sadly. "Well, then I suppose you think I'm

some kind of freak."

"No," he said with a casual shrug. "Unless you

think I'm some kind of freak."

He pointed to a small pile of leaves and twigs, and

suddenly a wisp of smoke ascended from them. A moment

later, a fire was burning, sending its warmth in Cat's

direction.

"You're a..." she began, astonished.

"A witch," he replied with a smile. "Well, I guess

I'm officially a warlock. I'm Donovan. Donovan

Farrington. And you're Catalpa Willoughby."

She nodded.

He reached out and wiped some of the rain drops from her face. Her heart pounded in her chest, and her eyes widened in surprise.

"And I think that you're the most beautiful girl in the school," he whispered.

Cat pulled her hand away from the stone as if she had been burned. She sat on the ground of the shelter, wrapped her arms around her legs, and wept for the love that might have been.

Chapter Fifteen

Finias waited until he heard Katie locking the front door before rising from his chair and glancing surreptitiously out his bedroom window. He watched Katie cross the parking lot and get into her small pickup truck, with the name of the Bed and Breakfast emblazoned on the side of the bed. He waited until she'd left the parking lot and drove down the street. Then, once she'd turned left at the light two blocks away, he felt safe enough to turn away from the window.

He hurried from his room and down to the end of the hall on the second floor. Sure enough, the door to the third floor Katie had mentioned was there, locked and secure. He examined the lock and smiled. It was aluminum and therefore did not contain iron which was an element that bound witches' abilities. He closed his hand around the lock and concentrated for a moment. The lock sprung open almost immediately.

He slipped the lock from inside the staple and placed it on a small side table in the hallway. Then he carefully opened the hasp, smiling as he noted that the door hardware was stainless steel and did contain iron. However, all he had to do was move it on its hinge for it to be rendered useless. No magic involved there.

Once the hasp was open, he turned the black porcelain knob on the door and slowly opened the door to the third floor.

Dust motes hung in the air as sunbeams worked their way through a threadbare curtain and grimy window. He looked at the wooden steps before him; they seemed stable enough. Ascending carefully, he tested each step as he went, holding on to the peeling handrail just in case.

When he reached the third floor, he stopped and closed his eyes, reaching inside himself to discern any abnormal energies around him. After a moment, he opened his eyes and walked to the double door at the end of the hallway. The doors had been painted white, but now the paint was peeling and exposing the original wood.

A chain was looped through the two door handles, and the chain was padlocked together. He picked up the lock and shook his head, steel this time. Then he looked at the chain and smiled; it was made of aluminum links. He slid his hand down to the middle of the chain, closed his eyes to concentrate, and the link opened in his hand. He unthreaded the chain from around the handles and pulled the door open.

Immediately, he was struck sideways by an invisible force and thrown across the large, all white room. He slammed into the wall and then jumped up, holding his hands in front of him for protection, gazing slowly around the room to find his attacker.

"Finias," the voice hissed, like an old snake. "My old friend."

"We were never friends," Finias replied, keeping himself on alert as he continued to scan the room to discern the source of the power.

"What a shame," the voice replied. "I could have made you rich. I could have given you whatever you desired."

"You know nothing of what I desire," Finias replied. "And you never have."

"You desire what all men desire," the demon mocked. "Money, power, and sex. That is how you were created, to lust after those basic needs."

"I'm afraid you are speaking about yourself," Finias said coolly. "Well, except for the sex part. It's kind of hard to have sex when you don't have a body."

Finias felt a slight movement of wind and was able to protect himself before the blow came. But even with the protection, he staggered back against the wall.

"When I kill those witches, I'll take your body, Finias," the demon threatened. "But I'll keep your spirit inside with me, so you can see the terror I will create with it. And after we kill them, perhaps we can go after others. How do you feel about children, Finias? Shall we start with some of them?"

Finias tamped down the rage building inside of him; the anger would only give the creature more power. He took a deep breath and moved away from the wall, slowly walking the perimeter of the room.

"I don't plan on allowing you to kill those witches," Finias explained, as he allowed his mind to continue to search the room.

"I hadn't planned on asking your permission," the demon answered. "However, if you would consider partnering with me…"

Finias chuckled softly, still walking slowly around the room, to pinpoint the location of the power. "I understand you already have a partner," he replied. "A young witch, much younger than me."

"How do you know that?" the demon seethed.

Finias stopped walking, now secure in his knowledge of the location of the energy. An old pipe about five feet above the floor, probably left there from when gas was used to light the old house, was the portal the demon was using to gain his entrance.

"You know who I am, and you know my abilities," Finias said, hoping to continue to distract the creature until he was ready. "Do you think I would enter a location without understanding who my allies and my foes were?"

"The young witch is weak," the demon replied. "He does not have the bloodlust I need for a true partner."

"I'm sure, at your hands, he will learn it," Finias said sadly.

Finias raised his hands and focused his power on the small pipe.

"Or, he will die," the demon said. "As will you, if you do not…"

"Exilium," Finias cried, pushing his power forward and across the room. Banishing the demon from the house.

The demon screamed, and the blood-curdling sound echoed throughout the room. But just as quickly as it began, the sound began to dissipate, like Finias' hands were on its throat, suffocating its power.

Finias held his hands in place until he could feel that there was no more evil energy in the room. With a long, deep breath, he focused once again. "Detorquere," he ordered, and the pipe in the wall twisted around, sealing the opening tightly.

He slumped back against the wall and breathed slowly, scanning the room for any other possible portals. Once he was satisfied there were no other places the creature could enter, he walked over to the pipe and drew some very old runes in the wall around the pipe, to bar the demon from coming back into the room again.

"Now, we can see…" he said to himself, then paused. He hurried across the room to the hallway and heard a vehicle pulling into the parking lot. He shook his head in frustration and then quickly pulled the chains back through the handles and sealed the room up once again. He quickly ran to the staircase and hurried down, replacing the lock into the hasp and staple, before he heard the rattle of a key on the outside door.

With a stealth that belied his size, he raced to his room and closed his door softly behind him. He leaned against the door and inhaled deeply. "Well, at least now he knows I'm in town," he mused. "Let the games begin."

Chapter Sixteen

"Donovan!"

Donovan sat straight up in his chair when he heard the demon scream his name inside his head. He looked at the others gathered around the table in the meeting room and was grateful that none of them could hear it.

"I need you now!"

He cleared his throat and then smiled apologetically to the partner making the presentation. "I'm so sorry," Donovan muttered. "I just remembered that I'd forgotten something in my office. I'll be right back. Please continue, I'll catch up."

He pushed back his chair and hurried out of the meeting room before anyone could question him. He jogged down the hallway, pushed open his office door, and then closed and locked it securely behind him.

"I told you to kill it!"

Donovan gasped as he felt his skin ripping beneath his shirt. "What?" he gasped. "What are talking about?"

"I told you there was an entity in this town, and I wanted you to kill it," the demon howled. "I gave you that direction yesterday."

"I haven't had time," Donovan answered. "I don't even know where he is."

"He's hot for the last witch," the demon sneered. "The one without a mate. He wants to have her."

Jealousy, pure and unadulterated, surged through Donovan's body, followed by rage. The influence of the demon filled his mind and took away all reason.

All he could see was Cat in the arms of a faceless stranger. Cat betraying his trust.

He was doing this for her! He was sacrificing for her! Why didn't she trust him?

"I guess you weren't enough for her," the demon taunted. "This one is strong. This one has power. This one will satisfy her needs."

"Where is he?" Donovan growled as the rage grew larger. He clenched his hands into fists. "I'll kill him now."

"Yes, you will," the demon encouraged. "But you will need more than your hands. You will need a gun."

Donovan nodded. "Yes, a gun," he agreed, his pupils now dilated and his movements slow and measured. "I need a gun."

"You are a witch," the demon reminded him. "Move a gun from the police department to your desk."

Donovan slowly smiled and nodded his head. Suddenly there was a heavy clattering sound coming from the desk in front of him. His smile widened. "I have a gun," he said obediently.

"Good. Very good," the demon rejoiced. "Now, why don't you call the Bed and Breakfast and ask to speak with Finias? See if he would be willing to meet you tonight."

Donovan picked up his phone and dialed the Bed and Breakfast.

"Hi, Katie speaking," he heard through his phone.

"Katie, this is Donovan," he replied, his voice still stiff.

"Are you okay?" she asked. "You don't sound like yourself."

"Long day," he improvised. "I was wondering if I could speak to Finias."

"Who?" she asked.

"Finias, he's staying at your B&B," Donovan insisted.

"Sorry, there's no one here by that name," Katie replied.

"She's a lying bitch," the demon's voice echoed in Donovan's brain.

"You're a…" Donovan began, nearly repeating the demon's words before catching himself. "Maybe my secretary got his name wrong. I was supposed to call a man staying at your B&B. He called me this afternoon when I was in a meeting."

"Oh, you must mean Ellis," Katie said. "Sorry, he stepped out just a few minutes ago."

"Oh, that's too bad," Donovan replied. "Do you know when he's going to be back?"

"No," Katie replied. "But I know he's going to Second Salem for dinner tonight. He asked me for directions and told me he was meeting some people there at six."

"Great," Donovan said. "I'll catch him there, thanks, Katie."

He hung up the phone and started to reach for the desk drawer with the gun.

"Oh, no, you don't need that until later," the demon coached. "Now you need to get back to your meeting. Then, after five, when everyone else is gone, you can get your gun and take it with you to meet Finias."

Donovan nodded, then turned around and walked out of his office. He started back down the hall toward the meeting room, his eyes going back to normal and his movements more natural. He'd nearly reached the meeting room when he froze. "What the hell just happened?" he asked himself, looking around the office. He stared back at his office door and shook his head. Did he even go into his office? He couldn't remember.

Man, I'm losing it, he decided silently. I need some down time. Maybe I'll head over to Second Salem's after work.

Chapter Seventeen

Agnes Willoughby stood at the foot of the path waiting for Cat's return. She smiled sadly, it hadn't been that long ago when she had taken the path up to the bluffs to seek answers about their future, and all three of her daughters had stood waiting for her, scolding her for going off without them. So much had changed in those few short months.

She sighed softly. Rowan had blossomed. Her love for Henry had not only given her faith in herself, but also courage in the research they'd done. And through that research, they had helped Joseph and his entire community. The vaccine Rowan created using samples from Joseph's blood, was reversing a disease that had wiped out most of the male population in their village. And now that Hazel was pregnant with Joseph's child... Agnes shook her head and wiped away the tears that sprang to her eyes.

Hazel, her baby, was going to be a mother. She shrugged, of course, it made perfect sense. Hazel had been a nurturer and a protector to her goats. For all of her sassy remarks and quips, she was the one who sensed hurt or frustration in her sisters. She would be a perfect mother.

"Which is going to make me a grandmother," Agnes whispered, and then she smiled. "A whole new generation to spoil and coddle, with none of the ramifications of parenthood."

Of course, she thought, she never really dealt with the ramifications of parenthood. She glanced up at the path. Catalpa had been born with a maturity and soberness that belied her years. She was the serious child, the responsible child, the child who reminded her mother of the duties required to run the household. Cat had been there for her sisters, and her mother, if Agnes was honest with herself. And now her beloved Cat was suffering, quietly suffering, because that's how she did things. But Agnes could feel her pain.

Agnes' thoughts were interrupted when she heard movement from beyond the first bend of the path, a place hidden behind the trees. A moment later, Fuzzy, her wolf and familiar, bounding into the clearing, looking over his shoulder to ensure he was being followed. Sure enough, moments later, Cat came into view.

"How was your walk?" Agnes asked softly, walking up to meet her daughter and enfold her in an embrace.

Cat relaxed into the embrace, feeling the love and support from her mom. Grateful for the strength it gave her and the courage to do what needed to be done. "Can I be honest?" Cat asked.

"I wish you would," Agnes replied.

Cat took a step back, her hands on her mother's shoulders. "I feel like a mail order bride," she said.

Agnes' eyes widened in surprise. "Wow, I wasn't expecting that at all," she replied. "Tell me more."

Cat sighed. "When you and I talked about the destiny of the Willoughby witches a couple of months ago, I was more than willing to do whatever it took to banish the demon," she explained. "And I still am. But this whole new requirement of giving my heart to a companion to help me. I don't know if I can do that. And I certainly don't want to be the weak link that sends my sisters to their death."

"Why can't you do it?" Agnes asked. "Is it that you can't trust another man?"

"I wish it were just that," Cat replied. "I just feel like I've already given my heart away. Even when Donovan left, and decided to pursue his other dreams, my heart never healed. I tried to date. I tried to meet other men. They were just never…"

"Donovan," Agnes finished.

Cat nodded. "Exactly," she said sadly. "I can't be responsible for his choices. I can't change him to be what I want him to be. But I wish I could heal myself so that I could love freely again."

"Maybe you just haven't met the right man," Agnes offered hopefully.

"Do you believe that?" Cat asked.

Agnes shook her head. "No. I don't," she said. She took her daughter's hand and led her to a giant tree trunk a few feet away from the path, and they both sat on it. Agnes took her daughter's hands in her own and then met her eyes.

"But let me tell you something that I hope will give you encouragement," Agnes offered. "Your father was the first man I ever loved. I gave him my heart, and he gave me his. Our time together was magical, and when I discovered I was pregnant with you, I was ecstatic and devastated."

"Because we had to be three from one," Cat said.

Agnes nodded. "Yes, my daughters had to come from three different fathers," she said. "And your father understood from the beginning that was what was required. We said goodbye…" Agnes closed her eyes. "It was so hard to leave him."

She opened her eyes, now moist with memories and smiled sadly. "I thought I was going to die," she admitted. "But I didn't. I had a beautiful baby girl, and I saw your father in you. And I knew together we had created a miracle."

She lifted her hand and gently caressed Cat's cheek. "You remind me of him every day," she confessed. Then she sighed. "And I realized that if I didn't cut off all contact from him, there would be no way that I could fulfill the rest of my responsibility."

"You never saw my father again?" Cat asked.

Agnes shook her head. "No, but I know he understood that we needed to be separated," she said. "At least I hoped he understood."

She paused for a moment and looked up to the pine forest, then turned back to Cat. "When I met Rowan's father, he was as different from your father as possible," she said. "And although it wasn't the same, deep love I had with your father, I still loved him. I loved his laughter; I loved his kindness. I loved the way his mind worked. And even though it wasn't as rich and deep as my love for your father, I could honestly say that I loved him. And I had that same kind of relationship with Hazel's father too."

She shrugged. "It wasn't as hard saying goodbye to the others," she confessed. "But there was a sweetness in each relationship."

She leaned forward and squeezed Cat's hands. "All I'm saying is that you can still love, even if it's not Donovan," she explained. "It's not going to be that powerful, all-consuming first love that you had with him, but there can be a sweet love and mutual respect and admiration with someone else."

"So, I don't have to lie to myself?" Cat asked. "Tell myself that it never was love with Donovan?"

Agnes shook her head. "No, you don't," she said. "Because it was true love and it was wonderful, if only for a little while. But now, your path, just like mine, needs you to walk away from Donovan and seek love with someone else."

Cat leaned forward and rested her head on her mother's shoulder. "It hurts," she whispered, and Agnes could hear the tears in her voice.

"I know, darling," Agnes said softly, rubbing her daughter's back tenderly. "I know."

Chapter Eighteen

Two hours later, her make-up applied, her hair dried and her dress laid out on the bed for her to slip into, Cat sat down on the thick carpet next to her bed and gracefully moved into the Lotus position. She rested her wrists lightly on her knees, touched the tips of her thumbs to her index fingers, and closed her eyes. She breathed in slowly and, at the same time, concentrated on releasing the tension from her body. She started at the top of her head, visualizing the tension washing down her body and out of her toes. She relaxed her brow, the cheeks, and nose, her mouth, her chin, and then her jaw. Slowly rotating her neck, she pushed the tension from the muscles and let her head fall forward, her chin touching her chest. Then she relaxed her shoulders, slowly moving them in clockwise and counter-clockwise circles to make them limber and free. She moved down, releasing the tension from the rest of her body and finally, in a state of complete relaxation, she slowed her mind to open to the energy around her.

"Let me see Donovan," she requested softly.

She could almost feel the ground move underneath her as her mind raced from the farmhouse to the nearby city of Whitewater. She could only see the blurry darkness of her trance-like state, but all of her other senses were alive and awake. She could smell the difference in the air, now filled with scents of the city replacing the fragrance of the herb meadows. She could hear the echo of sound off the buildings. Could feel the rush of people around her.

Finally, she arrived at his office building, and the scents, sounds, and atmosphere changed. She concentrated on only Donovan and her progress slowed. Finally, she knew she was in the same room as him. She took a deep breath and concentrated on his thoughts.

Her mind moved closer to his, but all she found was a solid wall of black. Her forehead furrowed in confusion. He'd never been able to totally block her before. She tried again, concentrating with more power. Still, the wall was there, keeping out his thoughts. She studied the wall and finally saw a tiny door on the far side. She moved toward it and began to reach out.

"You do not want to open that."

She jumped back as if she had been burned, and then her mind focused on the voice. It was the same shadowy figure from her meditation this morning, the same spirit guide who had been with her all of her life.

"Why not?" she asked.

"It is not Donovan," he said. "It was placed there, in his mind, to frighten you."

"Who? Who could do that?" she gasped.

"You know who," he said. "But I will not say his name aloud; it only gives him more power. Do you understand."

She nodded. She turned from him to look back at the door and gasped when she saw a trickle of bright, red blood flow from the bottom corner of the door down the white wall.

"Whose blood?" she stammered.

The shadow moved and blocked her sight. "You must not see this!"

"I need to know if he's hurt," she insisted. "I need to know if I can help him."

"This is not about Donovan," the guide insisted. "This is only to frighten you."

"You can't know that for sure," she argued. "You can't guarantee that I won't be able to help."

His sigh echoed in her mind, a combination of sadness and frustration. "No, I cannot know for sure," he said. "But I know of its ways, and I am sure it is a trap."

She took a moment to ponder her decision. Donovan would not have closed his mind to her; she wouldn't believe that. He wouldn't have allowed the demon to have gained that much control over him; he knew better. This was a trick. A trick by the demon. A trick to keep her from discovering how she could actually help Donovan.

"I choose to look," she finally announced.

He stepped to the side, and her way was no longer blocked.

She moved ahead, reached out, and opened the door.

The naked bodies were sprawled on top of an altar of black stone, their arms and legs draped over the side. A hooded creature hovered over them, closest to the one on the end. She moved closer, quietly, so the creature could not hear her.

The sounds coming from the creature were guttural and fragmented, combined with soft slurping sounds. Confused, she moved even closer.

Then she noticed. The bodies. Their bodies. Rowan, Hazel, Mom… Her horror increased as she recognized the last body, the body the creature was hovering over, as her own. She cried out softly; the pain of vision wounded her heart.

The creature heard. The noises stopped. The movement stilled. And the creature lifted its hooded head and stared up at her.

Donovan.

She shook her head in disbelief.

He smiled at her and allowed a trickle of her own blood to drip from his mouth down his chin.

"Hello, Cat!"

She screamed, the sound echoing throughout the house, as she pulled herself back. Back through the tiny door, back away from Donovan's mind, back from the office building, back from Whitewater and finally back to the safely of her room.

Chapter Nineteen

Hazel and Rowan burst through Catalpa's bedroom door and rushed to her side. Hazel kneeled in front of her, her arms wrapped around her older sister while Rowan placed her hands on Cat's head to see if she'd been hurt.

"She's been traveling," Hazel said to Rowan. "But I think she's coming back."

Cat shook and then gasped as her eyes opened. For a moment, she didn't know where she was and tried to push herself out of Hazel's arms, but Hazel held her tightly. "It's me Cat," she whispered. "You're safe. You're home."

Cat shook violently and then started to weep, collapsing against her sister. Hazel just held her, and Rowan knelt next to them and wrapped her arms around Cat too. "We're both here," Rowan soothed. "And nothing can harm you anymore."

For a few minutes, the sisters knelt in silence, letting Cat weep for as long as needed, then Cat took a deep, shuddering breath and faced her sisters. "I saw our deaths," she stammered, wiping the tears from her face with her hands. "And I saw Donovan…"

She trembled and took another deep breath. "He was…he was like a vampire," she choked. "And he was drinking my blood."

"Where did you see this?" Rowan asked.

"I wanted to check on Donovan," Cat explained, her voice still shaky. "But his thoughts were blocked, except for a small door."

"That doesn't make sense," Hazel said. "Donovan's always been open to you."

Cat nodded. "I know," she agreed. "So, when my spirit guide warned me…"

"Wait, your spirit guide warned you?" Rowan asked. "What did he say?"

Cat took another deep breath and wiped the remaining moisture away. "He said it was a trick to frighten me," she confessed. "He said it was the…" She paused as she tried to remember the word.

"The mosquito," Hazel inserted. "It was a trick by the mosquito."

"Yes," Cat said. "That he set it there for me, knowing that I would try and look at Donovan's thoughts."

"And so, you entered the trap," Rowan said. "And he caught you, hook, line, and sinker."

"No, that's not how it went," Cat argued. "We…all of us…were dead. Laying on a stone altar."

"With a vampire drinking our blood," Hazel added, rolling her eyes. "It sounds like a really bad horror flick. I can't believe you fell for it."

"Wait! I'm the incredibly frightened sister here," Cat announced. "You are supposed to be sympathetic."

"Yeah, well sympathy lasted for about three minutes until we found out you were stupid," Hazel replied.

"I am not stupid!" Cat exclaimed.

"No?" Rowan asked. "What if one of us had decided to take a little astral plane walk into the mind of someone and were stopped and warned by our spirit guide but disregarded what he said because we thought we knew better. What would you call us?"

Cat paused for a moment and then nodded slowly. "Stupid," she agreed.

"The mosquito must be pretty worried about losing if he had to create a vision like that, just to scare us," Hazel said, hugging her sister. "And, he must be worried about your influence over Donovan to create a wall that blocks you."

"He did frighten me," Cat agreed, taking a deep breath. "And now I'm pissed. Mostly because I fell for it, but partly because he really scared the crap out of me."

"We can't let him have that kind of power over us," Rowan said. "We can't let fear enter this equation because fear destroys hope."

"You're right," Cat said. "You're right. I should have listened to my spirit guide."

"He's never been wrong before," Hazel added. "Remember when he gave you dating advice?"

Cat smiled and nodded. "Don't trust any boys, ever, at all," she laughed. "He must have been someone's Dad before he became my guide."

Rowan laughed. "Here I had advice from Patience Goodfellow about proper manners and etiquette," she teased. "And you had someone who must have been a warrior who guided you. I have to admit that sometimes, I was jealous."

"He has been like a warrior, hasn't he?" Cat admitted, feeling calm enough to laugh. "But, I guess, with my gifts I needed someone like a drill sergeant to instruct me. Poor Patience would have thrown up her arms in frustration if she had to guide me."

Hazel leaned back, plucked a tissue from a box on Cat's nightstand and handed it to her. "So, you have about twenty minutes before we have to leave," she said. "So, take a moment to apologize to your guide, and then go fix your makeup because…dang!"

Cat smiled. "That bad, huh?"

Hazel grinned. "Let's just say that it's a good thing you have twenty minutes," she teased.

Rowan gave Cat a quick hug. "Don't listen to her," she said. "You'll knock him off his feet as soon as you walk in the door."

Smiling, Cat waited until her sisters left the room before she closed her eyes and sought her guide.

Chapter Twenty

It took only a few moments for Cat's spirit guide to appear, shadowy and tall, in the peripheral of her mind.

"How are you?" he asked, his voice filled with concern.

"Feeling stupid," she admitted. "But otherwise fine."

"That was a terrifying vision to see," he replied. "And it will remain in your memory to haunt you unless you face it again."

She shook her head. "I can't face it again," she whispered, her voice trembling.

"You and I will face it together," he said. "But we will not go to Donovan's mind to see it, we will see it from your memory."

She felt his support as if it were a tangible touch, and she nodded. "Now?" she asked. "I have a date…"

"A date?" he asked. "In the midst of a war, you have a date?"

She shrugged. "According to the grimoire, I must find a companion that will help dispel the demon," she explained. "So, it's more of a meeting of mutual forces than a date."

She heard his soft chuckle. "Ah, so it is a strategic meeting of minds and talents," he teased. "A war plan."

"I suppose so," she admitted.

"Will you be able to concentrate on the plan if we don't vanquish the memory first?" he asked.

She thought about it for a moment. "I might actually be more focused on the plan with the memory still fresh in my mind," she replied. "I'm pretty pissed off that the demon did this to me."

"Good! I am glad to see that you are angry and not frightened," he said with enough pride in her that she smiled. "That's my warrior!"

"So, we can wait?" she asked.

"Yes, we can wait until tonight," he agreed. "But no later, I do not want you to have nightmares from your experience. Your subconscious will want to play with this new memory, and we have to direct it to give you power, not fear."

Cat nodded. "I understand," she said. "And thank you."

"For allowing you to go on your date?" he asked, confused.

She shook her head. "No, for trying to warn me in the first place," she said. "And not criticizing me for not listening to you in the second place."

"I would protect you from sorrow and fear if I could," he said. "But I understand that there are some things you must learn on your own."

"I know," she agreed. "I get to choose."

"Yes, you get to choose your actions," he agreed. "But you must remember that the consequences that follow along are not something that can be chosen."

Cat smiled. "You were someone's dad, weren't you?"

There was a long pause, and, finally, the spirit guide responded. "I beg your pardon."

Cat laughed softly. "Sometimes you sound like someone's dad," she replied. "And I'm grateful for that and the advice you've given me."

"You are welcome, Catalpa," he replied gently. "Now, get ready for your date and try to enjoy yourself."

"Thank you," she said. "I will."

Chapter Twenty-one

Cat parked her car in the spot next to Joseph's vehicle and took a deep breath. With her hands still on the steering wheel, she glanced up at the rearview mirror and took a good look at herself. Her makeup was fine, and her hair was in place, but there were definite signs of fear in her eyes. She was being ridiculous; this is only a date. A date at a local restaurant where she knew everyone. This was not the end of the world.

Then why was her stomach tied up in knots, and why were her palms sweaty?

The tapping on her window startled her, and she turned to see Hazel staring in at her. She rolled down the window.

"Did you want us to order drive-thru for you?" Hazel asked. "Or are you coming in?"

"Funny," Cat replied sarcastically. "I'm coming. I just had to psyche myself up."

"Are you psyched up enough now?" Hazel asked. "Because I'm starving, and the smell of the homemade potato chips is making my mouth water."

"What if I don't like him?" she asked her sister.

Hazel shrugged. "Well, if you don't like him, order the house salad," she suggested. "It's small, and you can eat it quickly. If you want to give him a chance, order the fish fry. It's all you can eat, so you can take your time."

With a long-suffering sigh, Cat rolled up the window and then slowly opened the car door while Hazel stepped out of the way. "I'm ready now," Cat said.

They entered the dimly lit restaurant, and Joseph glanced around. "There he is," he said, pointing to a corner booth. "Follow me."

The lighting was too dim and the restaurant too crowded for Cat to get a good look at the man waiting for them at the booth, so she followed behind Joseph and Hazel. When they reached the booth, Finias stood up and stepped to the side of the table, addressing Cat first.

"Hello," he said with a cordial smile. "I'm Ellis. Ellis Thomas."

Cat stared at him for a moment, a little overwhelmed by both his size and his unusual appearance. Finally, she smiled back. "I'm Catalpa Willoughby," she said, a little breathlessly. "My friends call me Cat."

"I hope that I will earn the honor to be considered a friend of yours," he replied, then he motioned to the bench he'd just vacated. "Please, be seated."

Cat nodded, sat on the seat, moving over to the far end, and then watched Ellis greet Joseph and Hazel with equal charm. She noticed that Joseph was friendly but still suspicious. But Hazel, on the other hand, was delighted with him.

"How did you get those amazing blue eyes with your dark skin?" Hazel asked. "They're almost mesmerizing."

Finias smiled at Hazel, but he seemed to Cat to be embarrassed about his looks. "I must give all the credit to my parents," he replied softly. "I had nothing to do with it."

"Well, your parents did a great job," Hazel laughed easily, moving into her seat. "And now that we have the introductions complete, we really should order some food."

"Of course," Finias replied, slipping into the bench next to Cat. He turned to her. "Are you familiar with the menu here? Do you know what you'd like? Some appetizers, perhaps?"

"We have to have some of the homemade chips," Hazel inserted. "With a side of cheese sauce. And then perhaps some of the soft pretzels with more cheese sauce."

Cat grinned. "What Hazel didn't mention is that she is pregnant and finally finding her appetite again," she explained quietly.

"Ah," Finias said with a knowing nod. "So, we should order quickly and generously."

Cat laughed, suddenly feeling at ease with him. "Right now, her eyes are much bigger than her stomach," she replied. "But quickly is a good idea."

Finias looked over and caught the attention of one of the waitresses, who, Cat noted, had been staring at him the entire time. She came over and smiled at him. "May I help you?" the waitress asked eagerly.

"I believe we need some appetizers, as quickly as possible," he said. "Could we get a large order of your homemade chips with cheese sauce, as well as some soft pretzels with cheese sauce and…" He looked at Hazel. "How do you feel about deep-fried cheese curds?"

She smiled and nodded. "I feel very good about those," she replied.

He looked at the waitress and added the cheese curds to the list. "If you wouldn't mind getting those going right away," he asked courteously. "We will be ready with our drink requests and dinner orders when you get back."

"Okay, I'll get the order in and be right back," she said.

Finias turned to Cat and smiled. Cat was surprised to feel a hint of camaraderie towards him. This was not what she expected at all.

"Now that we've taken care of quickly and generously," he said softly, "What would you like to order?"

She smiled and quickly glanced at Hazel for a moment. "I'll have the fish fry," she said.

Chapter Twenty-two

Donovan walked back to his office after the meeting, his mind on the new responsibilities his boss had just given him. He was moving up in the firm and getting more opportunities. Whistling happily, he reviewed the last thirty minutes in the meeting. Yeah, this was good. Things were going really well for him at work.

He paused at his office door, his hand on the door knob, and a fleeting memory darted through his mind. He saw himself opening the door and rushing into the room early that afternoon. Shaking his head, he removed his hand from the door knob and stared at it.

"That can't be right," he whispered, running his hand through his hair. "I was in meetings all afternoon. I didn't come back to my office."

He closed his eyes for a moment and took a deep breath. He was imaging things that didn't happen. He was losing his mind.

"Okay, I need some down time," he said, opening the office door and walking inside. "I need some food, some friends and maybe a beer."

He walked over to his desk, put down his laptop, and picked up his phone. He dialed Cat's phone and waited, but after ringing a few times, he was directed to her voicemail. He hung up without leaving a message and called the Willoughby house. After two rings, Agnes answered.

"Donovan, it's so great to hear from you," Agnes said immediately. "How are you doing?"

"I'm great, Agnes," he replied. "How are you?"

"Well, you know, we're all on edge a little with all that's going on," she replied.

"Yeah, I can imagine," he replied. "It's harvest time, isn't it?"

There was a long moment of silence.

"Yes, it is harvest time," Agnes replied slowly. "And that keeps us pretty busy."

"I was just wondering if Cat was home," he said. "Can she drag herself away from the store?"

"Um, Donovan, we closed the store," Agnes reminded him.

He looked down at his watch. "Oh, yeah, jeez, it's after six, isn't it?" he replied, not understanding her comment. "Well, then, can I speak with her?"

"I'm afraid she's gone out with Hazel," she replied. "I'm so sorry. Do you want me to give her a message?"

Donovan shook his head as he pulled his office drawer open without thought. "No. No, that's okay," he replied casually. Looking across the room, toward the window, he robotically reached into the drawer, pulled the gun out, and stuffed it into his waistband underneath his suit jacket. "I'm just going to go out and get some dinner. I'll try her again tomorrow."

"Okay, Donovan," Agnes replied. "You take care of yourself."

He smiled and gently pushed the drawer closed. "I will, thanks," he said. "Have a good night."

"You too," she replied.

He shrugged and buttoned his suit jacket unconsciously. "Oh, yeah, I will."

Chapter Twenty-three

Joseph leaned back against the upholstered booth and scanned the restaurant. As a law enforcement officer, he automatically chose a seat where he could see the pub's door and watch who was coming and going.

Hazel leaned against him. "Are your spidey-senses kicking in?" she whispered.

He looked down at her in mock outrage. "Excuse me," he whispered back. "I have finely tuned canine intuitive abilities, not a bug's radar."

She giggled and wrapped her arm through his. "Oh, forgive me," she laughed. "How thoughtless of me."

She started to reach for another cheese curd when she saw Donovan enter the pub out of the corner of her eye. "Oh, incoming," she said.

"What?" Catalpa asked her sister, trying to look over her shoulder.

"Donovan just walked in," Hazel said. "And it looks like he's headed this way."

Joseph studied Donovan and felt a chill run down his back. "Something's off," he said, moving to block Hazel. "Something's wrong with him."

"What?" Hazel asked, leaning around him.

Reacting to Joseph's alarm, Finias turned around in the booth and then stood up. He looked at Donovan, and their eyes met. A satisfied smile appeared on Donovan's face as he moved toward the table and nodded at Finias.

"His eyes," Cat exclaimed. "His eyes are black."

Suddenly, Donovan reached into his suit jacket, pulled out the gun and aimed it at Finias.

"Bacainn!" Hazel shouted the Celtic word for barrier a moment before they heard the gun discharge. The single bullet slammed against the invisible barrier, causing waves of energy to reverberate from the contact point. Then the bullet ricocheted back, striking Donovan in the chest.

Donovan was propelled backwards by the force of the impact and collapsed onto the floor of the restaurant.

133

"Imeacht," Hazel ordered, removing the barrier as quickly as it had appeared.

"Donovan," Cat cried, climbing out of the booth and running to his side. She touched her hand to his neck and cried with relief. "He's still alive," she wept.

Joseph knelt on the other side of Donovan and saw blood staining Donovan's shirt. "We need to get him to a hospital," he said.

"I can help him," Finias said softly, and then he glanced around. "But I don't need an audience."

"I can do that," Cat replied, sniffing the tears back. She took a deep breath, closed her eyes, and recited the spell.

Like the shadows in the night,

Or the creatures lost from sight.

Bring invisibility,

As I ask, so mote it be.

Suddenly the restaurant around them faded into soft shadows. "We're good," she said. "No one can see us."

Finias placed his hands on Donovan's chest and gasped aloud.

"What?" Cat asked.

"I can stop the bleeding here," he said, and she could hear a strain in his voice. "But he needs more help than I can give him."

"Rowan and Henry could help," Hazel said. "I'll contact them."

Finias looked questioningly at Cat. "My sister and her fiancé," Cat explained. "Both remarkable healers."

Finias nodded. "Have them meet us at the Bed and Breakfast," he said. "I'll be able to move him there without too much pain."

Cat put her hand on his arm. "Pain for you, or him?" she asked.

He smiled down at her. "I'm afraid there will be pain for both of us," he replied. "But I will be careful with your friend."

She shook her head. "He isn't my friend," she said sadly. "Not anymore."

He nodded. "Well, let's just wait and see, shall we?"

Closing his eyes, he put his hands over the wound and concentrated, binding the nicked artery and closing the wound. His forehead was beaded with perspiration when he finally opened his eyes. "We can move him," he whispered.

Joseph nodded. "What about all of the witnesses?" he asked.

"I took care of that," Cat said. "They won't remember anything about the shooting, and they'll all remember us getting up together and leaving after dinner."

"Thank you," Joseph said, then he turned to Joseph. "Carry or have Hazel send him there?"

"It's only a few blocks away," Finias said. "I think we need to carry him, the ride through the ether might be too much for him."

"Rowan and Henry are on their way," Hazel said. "And there's an ambulance waiting outside the restaurant."

Cat turned and stared at her. "What?"

Hazel smiled and shrugged. "I'll return it when we're done," she replied, giving her sister a quick hug. "I figured we needed it just as badly as anyone else."

Cat smiled and wiped the tears from her eyes. "Thank you," she said.

"Just don't tell Mom," Hazel replied softly.

Chapter Twenty-four

Cat sat in the back of the ambulance, holding Donovan's hand and praying quietly as it traveled down the street. His face was pale and drawn, dark circles surrounded his eyes, and his face was contorted in a grimace of pain.

"Please," he groaned softly.

"What darling?" she whispered, bending over to better hear him.

Finias, sitting on the other side of the Donovan, widened his eyes at the term of endearment that came so easily from Cat's lips. "Be careful," he cautioned her.

She turned her head and glanced at him. "Why?" she asked, confused. "There's nothing he can…"

"Cat," Donovan rasped. "Cat, are you here?"

She immediately turned her attention back to Donovan, gently stroking the side of his face with her hand. "Yes. Yes, I'm here."

His eyes flew open, the irises solid black, and he smiled widely as he ran his tongue slowly across his lips. His hand clamped, like a steel grip, on her arm. "I'm going to drink every drop of your blood," he hissed. "And then I'm going to burn your body as a sacrifice to my Master."

Horrified, she pulled back, but he wouldn't let her go. She struggled against the grip on her arm. "Let me go," she cried, fighting with him. "Damn it, let me go!"

Finias laid his hand over hers and shook his head. "It's not him," he said with quiet assurance. "Donovan's not speaking to you. His body has become a conduit for the demon. Which is why I needed more help to heal him."

He placed his other hand on Donovan's face and gently closed his eyes. Cat's arm was immediately released, and Donovan moaned in agony. Looking down at her arm, she saw a red welt where Donovan's hand had been.

"Allow me," Finias said, placing his hand on Cat's arm.

She could feel the healing warmth not only repair the damage on her arm, but she felt reassurance fill her heart. Eyes brimming with tears, she looked up at him. "Why?" she asked.

He smiled tenderly. "We cannot always choose the direction of our hearts," he replied. "And I do not think we should be punished for loving too much."

She nodded, her throat too constricted with tears to speak.

He gently released her arm and then sat back against the wall of the ambulance. "Do you know Katie, the owner of the Bed and Breakfast?" he asked casually.

Cat nodded and cleared her throat. "I do," she finally replied.

"Good, because I'll need you to distract her somehow while we get Donovan up to the second floor," he said.

She felt the ambulance turning into the parking lot, grabbed hold of the stabilizing bar, and stood up. "Let me go in first," she said. "Then give me a couple of minutes before you bring him up."

"Thank you," Finias said.

She shook her head. "No, thank you," she replied. "For understanding."

She slipped out the back of the ambulance and jogged toward the front door of the B and B.

"I understand far more than you realize," Finias said under his breath. Then he looked down at the unconscious Donovan. "And now, young man, you need to fight with everything you've got because this isn't going to be easy."

Chapter Twenty-five

Cat opened the door to the B and B and quickly glanced around. The front lobby, the sitting room, and the dining room were all empty. Could they have been lucky enough to find the place empty? Then she noticed a light in the back of the house, pooling out from underneath the swinging door to the kitchen. She hurried in that direction.

"Katie," she called, keeping her voice friendly and neutral. "Katie, are you back here?"

She pushed the door open and found Katie at the kitchen counter, watching a Youtube video on cooking and trying to emulate the steps. Katie glanced over her shoulder and smiled at Cat. "Cat! Hi," she said, her hands caked in dough. "This is a nice surprise."

Cat let the door close behind her and then with a quick spell, sealed the kitchen in a sound-proof barrier. "I was in town on some other errands, and I wanted to stop by and see if there was anything you needed from the store," Cat said. "I didn't mean to disturb you."

Katie shook her head and then blew a random piece of hair off her face. "No, not a problem," she said. "As a matter of fact, I was going to call you and place an order. My guests can't live without your family's jams and preserves."

Cat smiled and tried to relax. "That's wonderful to hear," she replied. "What are you making?"

"Oh, it's brioche," Katie replied. "I wanted to make French Toast for breakfast."

"That sounds amazing," Cat said. "I'm sure your guests will love it."

Katie sighed. "I sure hope so," she said. "And I hope they remember it when they write their reviews."

Cat nodded sympathetically. "It's all about the reviews, isn't it?" she asked as she glanced out the window just in time to see the ambulance disappear. With a relieved exhale, she turned back to Katie. "I just remembered another errand I have. Would you mind if I called you for that list?"

"Oh, actually, that would be great," Katie said. "I still have to knead the dough for a while."

Cat backed up towards the door. "Well, let me know how your brioche turns out," she said.

"If you'd like, you can stop by tomorrow morning and have some," Katie offered. "I know I'll make more than enough."

Cat nodded and smiled. "I might take you up on that. Have a good night."

She quickly slipped out of the room, ensuring that the barrier was still intact, and hurried to the staircase. Just as she stepped onto the first step, the door opened behind her. She turned, poised to fight, and breathed a sigh of relief when she saw it was Rowan and Henry.

"We came…" Rowan started in her normal tone.

"Shhhh!" Cat cautioned, glancing back toward the kitchen to make sure the door didn't open.

"Sorry," Rowan replied, lowering her voice. "We came as quickly as we could."

"They're upstairs," Rowan whispered back.

"Donovan…" She stopped, tamped down the emotion, and tried again. "Donovan tried to shoot us."

"What?" Henry exclaimed softly.

"Hazel put up a barrier, and the bullet ricocheted back into Donovan," Cat continued. "Ellis tried to heal him…"

"Ellis?" Rowan asked.

"My blind date," Cat replied. "But he said he needed more help. Come on; I was causing a distraction for them with Katie, so I haven't been upstairs yet."

Cat went up the stairs, followed closely by Rowan and Henry.

"Is it just a bullet wound?" Henry whispered.

Cat shook her head. "No, Ellis feels that Donovan is some kind of conduit for the demon," she replied. "He said he needed more help."

"So, he's possessed?" Henry asked.

Cat froze on the stairs, and the other two nearly walked into her. She turned, her eyes wide with fear.

"Possessed?" she asked, her voice thick with terror. "Do you really think…"

Rowan shook her head and stepped up to place her arm around her sister's waist. "We have no idea what's wrong yet," she said in placating voice. "So, it does us no good to speculate. Henry just does that because he's a professor and they have to create hypotheses and presumptions. It's how his mind works."

She shot an apologetic glance over her shoulder at her fiancé, and he winked back.

"But… if he's possessed," Cat stammered as they reach the second floor.

"Then we'll just have to unpossess him," Henry said, stepping over to the other side of Cat and placing his hand on her shoulder. "Don't worry. We'll save your Donovan."

Cat smiled up at him. "Thank you," she said. She stepped away from them and walked through the slightly ajar door.

Rowan put her hand on Henry's chest before he could follow Cat. "Can we save him?" she asked. "Are you sure?"

Henry shook his head. "I really hope so."

Chapter Twenty-six

Agnes Willoughby stood in front of the sink in the kitchen, looking out the window at the backyard. She tapped her fingers impatiently against the soapstone farmhouse sink as she gazed outside, hoping that one of her children would either return home or call her and let her know what the hell was going on!

She glanced at her phone laying on the soapstone counter next to the sink and shook her head. No! She was not going to call them. She wasn't going to interrupt them when they were doing something important. She wasn't going to be that kind of mother.

She started to reach for her phone.

"Ruff!"

Agnes jumped and then looked down at Fuzzy. "I wasn't going to call," she lied. "I was going to check the weather, that's all." She leaned over the sink and looked up into the evening sky. "Looks like rain. That's what I was thinking. Rain."

The wolf yawned loudly and shook its head.

"I am so not lying," Agnes replied. "You're just overly suspicious."

The wolf stood up and walked over to the back door, then looked back at her.

"Oh, so you are just as worried as I am," she said, walking over to join him.

Whining softly, the wolf leaned against the door.

"Fine," Agnes said, reaching for the doorknob and opening the door. "You can go out. But no running into the fields, you need to stay with me."

The wolf loped down the stairs and into the back yard. Agnes followed him out of the house and stood on the deck, watching him. She glanced over at the protective runes on the posts at the top of the staircase, and a shudder went through her body. She wrapped her arms around herself and took a step back, toward the door.

"Fuzzy," she called. "Are you done?"

Just then a large crow swooped down and landed on the cast iron dinner bell that was on a post at the foot of the stairs. The crow flapped its wings a few times as it settled on the top of the bell and finally roosted.

"Fuzzy," Agnes called, her voice urgent with concern. "You need to come in now."

The crow turned and looked at her. "Worried Agnes?" it hissed.

"Get the hell off of my property," she commanded, tightening her grip on her arms so she wouldn't shake. "Get out now!"

"Oh, Agnes, I thought we could try and be friends," the crow continued. "After all, if we could come to some agreement, then your daughters won't have to die."

"My daughters won't die," Agnes replied, a sick feeling twisting her stomach. "But you will be sent back to the hell you came from."

"I've already tasted their blood," the crow taunted. "It was delicious."

"You lie!" Agnes shouted at him.

"You heard about the shooting at the pub, didn't you? Poor Donovan was crazy out of his mind with jealousy," it continued. "Poor Cat, lying in a pool of her own blood." The crow turned and smiled. "Delicious blood."

"No!" Agnes screamed and ran forward towards the stairs.

Suddenly, a blur of fur crashed into her body, knocking both of them against the kitchen door. "What are you...?" she screamed at the wolf and then she saw the determination in the wolf's eyes.

She took a deep, shuddering breath when she realized she had nearly allowed herself to move out of the protection of the runes — nearly fallen for the demon's trap.

"I'm sorry, Fuzzy," she sobbed, burying her face in the wolf's fur.

Fuzzy nuzzled her and then turned, putting himself between the crow and Agnes. He stepped to the edge of the porch, bared his teeth and growled viciously.

"Order your wolf to attack, Agnes," the crow taunted. "I would love to disembowel him and scatter his parts across the yard."

Fuzzy continued to growl and stand between them.

Agnes wiped the back of her hand impatiently across her face, pushing away the tears. She stood up, took a deep breath, and then walked across the deck to the wicker table and chairs. Lying on the table was a super soaker water-gun. She picked it up, pumped the piston, and then walked back to stand alongside Fuzzy.

The crow lifted its head and laughed. "Really, Agnes, you're going to shoot me with a squirt gun?" it mocked.

Agnes lifted it, aimed, and shot a stream of water at the bird.

The crow screamed in pain, and red welts appeared on its body, and the odor of burning flesh filled the air.

"Did I neglect to mention this was holy water?" Agnes asked, pumping the piston again. "How forgetful of me."

She shot the gun again, but the crow took to the air, cawing in pain as it flew away from their property. Agnes dropped one hand on the top of Fuzzy's head. "Thank you," she whispered, her voice shaking. "You probably saved my life."

Fuzzy leaned against her and whined softly. She chuckled softly. "Yes. Yes, you can have a treat," she agreed. "You can have a damn ribeye if you'd like."

With his tail wagging excitedly, Fuzzy led her back to the kitchen door and barked loudly. "You're right," she agreed. "I deserve a treat too."

She opened the door, they both walked in, and she locked it securely behind them. "But first," she said with a long, shaky exhale. "I think I need just to sit down before my knees give out on me."

Chapter Twenty-seven

When Cat entered the bedroom, she saw that Donovan was still lying on a gurney and not on the queen-sized wrought iron bed in the middle of the room. She glanced over to Finias, a question in her eyes and he nodded. "I thought it would be better to keep him on a surface that's more accessible," he said quietly.

She came closer and noted that his wrists and ankles had been strapped to the edges of the gurney to keep him immobilized. Why in the world were they tying him up? Was this some kind of punishment for his earlier attack?

"Are we worried that he's going to run away?" she asked skeptically.

Finias started to answer Cat, then saw Rowan and Henry enter the room and stopped. "I'm glad you're here," he said to them. "I'd like to see what you think before we start."

He bent over and whispered a few soft words in Donovan's ear.

"What are you doing?" Cat demanded.

Finias glanced up at her. "He has a glamour spell over him," he said. "I am merely reversing the spell."

"Why would he put a glamour spell…" Rowan began, then gasped in horror as she looked at the change in Donovan's body. His skin was pale and mottled with bruises; his eyes were surrounded by dark circles, his lips were chapped and were a light purple color.

"What's happened to him?" Cat cried softly, looking up at Finias.

"If I'm not mistaken," Finias said. "This is not all of his injuries." With a sweep of his hand over Donovan's torso, Donovan's bloodied suit jacket and shirt were removed. The red puckered bullet wound was visible in his right shoulder, but that wasn't what drew Cat's eyes. Donovan's entire torso was riddled with oozing and swollen gashes that were over twelve inches long. Yellow, putrid discharge seeped from the edges of the wounds and

155

coagulated around the gashes. His skin was stretched tightly over his ribcage, and the flesh that wasn't scarred was bruised.

"I've seen this before," Finias explained. "Although not so severe as this."

Henry stepped closer and nodded. "Demon possession," he said sadly.

"No!" Cat argued. "No. Donovan would never…"

"Donovan thought he could control it," Joseph said, interrupting her. "Donovan thought he could offer himself to the demon, get it to trust him, and then destroy it from the inside."

"Instead, it destroyed him," Hazel sobbed, turning her face into Joseph's shoulder to block her view.

Cat took a deep breath and shook her head. "No, it did not destroy him," she said firmly. "I would know, in my heart, if he was truly lost."

Finias looked at her and nodded. "What would you have us do?" he asked her.

"We need to save him," she said.

"There's a lot of danger in doing this," Henry inserted.

Cat spun and looked at him. "Really? We're worried about danger?" she cried. "What if this was Rowan lying here? Would you worry about danger then?"

Henry looked like he'd been struck. Finias reached over and took Cat's hands in his. "Cat, Henry was talking about danger to Donovan," he said quietly.

Tears rolled down Cat's face, and she nodded silently, trying to find the words, but unable to speak. "I'm sorry," she sobbed. Finias drew her into his arms to comfort her, but she stepped back. She placed her hand on his shoulder and smiled up at him. "Thank you, but I need…"

She wiped away the tears and turned to Henry.

"I'm so sorry," she apologized. "I know…"

Henry smiled at her. "I understand," he said. "We're all a bit overwhelmed at the moment."

"We need a plan," Rowan said. "That's what we need. And we need to understand why healing Donovan is dangerous."

"Donovan needs to want the demon to be gone," Henry said. "Because if he allows it to return, it will be worse."

"What?" Cat asked.

"When the unclean spirit is gone out of a man, he walketh through dry places, seeking rest, and findeth none," Finias quoted. "Then he saith, I will return into my house from whence I came out; and when he is come, he findeth it empty, swept, and garnished. Then goeth he, and taketh with himself seven other spirits more wicked than himself, and they enter in and dwell there: and the last state of that man is worse than the first."

"Seven times the possession," Henry said. "If he's not ready to give it up."

Chapter Twenty-eight

"Look at what it's doing to him," Cat said, shaking her head in disbelief. "How can you not believe that he's ready to give it up?"

"I've seen addicts in even worse shape than Donovan, and they didn't want to give it up," Joseph said.

"But this isn't an addiction," she argued. "This was a sacrifice. He did it for us." Her voice broke. "He did it for me."

"Maybe, he started out doing it for you," Joseph said. "But he got pulled in. I talked to him earlier this week, and for an instant, he was enjoying the power it gave him. I'm not saying that was his motivation, but he's got to be sure."

Cat turned to Finias. "You said you'd seen this before," she said. "What did you do? What can we do?"

"We can first heal the body," Finias replied. "Although, we risk when we heal the body because we make the entire entity stronger. There is a reason his body looks as it does, the body is holy, the body is spiritual; when it is attacked by evil; it will reject it. We are contradicting the body's natural response to the demon."

"But he can't choose until he's conscious," Cat insisted. "Until he's better."

Finias met her eyes. "And if he makes the wrong choice, are you ready to destroy him?" he asked. He stared at her and asked again, his voice a harsh whisper. "If we cure the body, but the spirit has decided to seek the power of the demon, are you willing to destroy Donovan?"

"Would he kill my sisters and my mother?" Cat asked, meeting his eyes unblinkingly. "Yes, I could, and I would destroy him. Without hesitation."

They all heard a weak cough and a soft chuckle. "That's my girl," Donovan wheezed. "Such a romantic."

They all turned to the man lying on the gurney.

"Donovan…" Cat began.

He twisted his arms and felt the bands restricting his movement. "Are these necessary?" he asked acerbically.

Joseph moved over so he could meet Donovan's eyes. "I don't know," he said. "You tell me. You walked into Second Salem and tried to shoot either Ellis or Cat; we're not sure which. And then on the way here, you told Cat that you wanted to drink her blood."

"What?" he breathed, insult replaced with remorse. "I don't…"

"You don't remember," Finias said. "Because you were not in control of your mind. Or your actions. So, do you want us to remove the bands?"

He shook his head. "No," he agreed vehemently. "And get iron, bind me with iron, just in case."

Cat shook her head. "No, we don't have to…"

But just as she was arguing, Hazel waved her hand and replaced the fabric bands with iron cuffs. "They're padded," Hazel quickly pointed out. "And, he's right, if someone else is controlling him, we can't be too cautious."

"Donovan, we want to heal as much as we can," Rowan said, moving up to the gurney and gently stroking

161

his hair from his forehead. "Some of the things we won't be able to fix because of your connection."

Donovan's eyes widened. "My connection," he breathed. "Can he hear this? Does he know? Are you at risk?"

"These are my rooms," Finias said. "I protected them as soon as I arrived. He will not be able to break through these barriers, which is why I wanted you brought here and not a hospital."

"Thank you," Donovan replied, then he turned to Rowan. The woman he thought of as a little sister. How could he put her at risk? How could he ask her to clean out something as vile as what filled him? "These wounds are filled with evil. I don't want you to take that in, even if it's just to expel it out again. Can't we just use salve or something?"

"Oh, yeah, Row," Hazel quipped, staring at Donovan in exasperation and rolling her eyes, "let's use that demon-out salve we have at the store. I totally forgot about that."

162

Rowan chuckled and shook her head. "I can do this, Donovan," she assured him. "I won't put anyone at risk, I promise."

Donovan sighed. "Okay, I'll leave myself in your capable hands," he said, then he turned to Finias. "What do you want me to do."

"You must fill your mind with visions of love and peace," Finias instructed. "Instances where you felt warm and safe."

Donovan met Cat's eyes, and she moved forward and slipped her hand into his. "Can I help him?" she asked.

Finias shook his head. "No, this is his journey, and he must do it with his own strength," he said. "But, your hand in his is a powerful talisman and reminder of good. So, keep it there. Just, no linking." He met her eyes. "Promise?"

She nodded.

Donovan closed his eyes and remembered the first time he felt accepted.

The rain had stopped, and the air smelled like wet soil, wet vegetation, and sunshine, a heady combination. But he was sad. He wanted it to rain forever so that Cat would be trapped in little rock shelter with him. Away from the world, away from reality.

He smiled at her again, and she smiled shyly back. He was amazed that she was still there. She had always reminded him of a timid forest creature with her large brown eyes and hesitant looks. Even in Whitewater, the Willoughbys had been ostracized, either because of fear or envy. But he knew, being the eldest sister, it had been hardest on Cat.

"It's stopped raining," she pointed out, blushing when she thought about what she'd said. "I guess you could see that too."

He nodded and looked out over the bluff. "I was kind of hoping it would last longer," he admitted.

Her smile brightened. "Me too."

They stood in silence for a few more moments.

"I know," she said suddenly. "You could walk me home." She shook her head, suddenly shy. "I'm sorry, I mean if you want to, you could."

Donovan shrugged. "Yeah, I don't know," he hedged.

Her smile disappeared. "No, that's okay," she said, shaking her head. "It was, you know, just a stupid idea."

She started to move past him, not meeting his eyes. He had hurt her feelings, he realized.

"Wait," he said, touching her shoulder.

She turned, and he saw her sadness. She shrugged. "I'm good, really."

"It just that people don't like me," he explained in a rush. "My folks, they were the wrong side of the track kind of people. Not like the Willoughbys."

"My mom would love you," Cat exclaimed with a smile.

And with all his heart, Donovan hoped that would be true.

Chapter Twenty-nine

"He's in a good place," Rowan said. "I can feel positive energy."

Henry nodded and placed his hands on Donovan's head. "Okay, where do we want to start?" he asked.

Rowan stepped up next to him and placed her hands on Donovan's shoulders. She looked up to Finias. "You have the most experience," she offered.

He placed his hands over Donovan's heart. "Let's start with the bullet wound," he suggested. "To make sure there isn't anything damaged in there. Then, let's examine his organs to see what damage has been done there. The skin is superficial." He smiled at Rowan. "We can use your demon-out salve for that."

She chuckled softly and nodded. "Good plan," she said.

They all closed their eyes and began their journey through Donovan's injured body. "His clavicle was missed, but he's got some damage to the subscapularis," Henry said. "I can repair that."

"He's so sexy when he talks like a professor," Rowan whispered, then she focused on the damage to Donovan's body. "The bullet's exit wound — looks like it nicked the suprascapular artery as well as the nerve. It looks like you repaired the artery, Ellis, so I'll repair the nerve."

"The path throughout looks clean," Finias said. "I don't see any fragments, so I'll close up the skin both front and back."

They all worked in silence for several minutes, pulling the pain and injury into their own bodies and releasing it into the universe. Finally, Rowan sighed. "Okay, I'm done," she said, her voice slightly weary. "I'm going to check his lungs while I'm in the neighborhood."

Henry nodded. "I'll check his abdominal area if you want to check his heart, Ellis," Henry suggested.

He was so busy concentrating on the wound, Finias didn't remember that he had told them his name was Ellis, so he didn't respond.

"Ellis," Henry repeated. "Did you hear me?"

"Oh! Of course," Finias finally replied. "Yes, I can do the heart."

"The lungs are basically good," Rowan said. "There's a little residue in the bronchioles that actually look like soot."

"I've seen that before," Finias responded. "Brimstone soot, it's sulfuric in nature."

"Are you kidding me?" Rowan asked. "As in fire and brimstone in the Bible?"

"Exactly," Finias said. "Although the Bible has been interpreted and changed over the years, it still contains many truths. How much is there?"

"Just a dusting," Rowan replied. "How should I deal with it?"

"It would be nice if we could contain it," Finias said. "Rather than release it into the atmosphere."

"I can help," Hazel said.

"No, you're pregnant," Joseph inserted. "I don't want you anywhere near that toxic stuff."

She reached up and kissed his cheek. "I don't have to be near it," she said. "I just have to link with Rowan, see what she's seeing, and move it somewhere. Let me transfer a beaker and lid from Rowan's laboratory here and then we can move it."

Donovan lay back in his self-hypnotic state, partly listening to the conversations around him, partly daydreaming.

"You do that, and I'll deal with his heart," Finias said.

My heart, Donovan thought lethargically, I have a good heart.

"He has a good heart," Agnes Willoughby said, as Donovan hid behind the door to the kitchen to eavesdrop on her conversation with Cat. He had learned in his young life that people rarely told you the truth to

170

your face, but once they stepped a few yards away, they would let loose.

"I think so too," Cat agreed. "And he was so nice to me."

"I like his eyes," Agnes added. "I like how he looks at me, without dissembling, and seems to be saying 'take me as I am.' That takes courage."

Donovan's eyes widened in surprise. He had been told that he was bold and arrogant, that he didn't know his place. No one had ever told him he had courage.

"He told me that his folks were from the wrong side of the track," Cat said.

Donovan started to feel betrayed, but then remembered he hadn't told her in confidence.

"The world's round," Agnes replied, as she filled up a plate with cookies. "There are no wrong sides of the track. Sooner or later, the sides join together."

Cat giggled. "I should tell him you said that," she said.

Agnes' voice softened, and Donovan leaned in closer to listen. This was when she was going to warn her daughter away from him; he just knew it.

"No, don't tell him that," Agnes said. "Just accept him for who he is and treat him like he is the best friend you ever had. Because, if you treat him like that, he will be."

And at that moment, Donovan vowed that he would be the best friend not just Cat, but the whole Willoughby family ever had.

Chapter Thirty

"This stuff is disgusting," Hazel said, peering at the closed container of brimstone soot. "Donovan had this in his lungs. How could he breathe?"

"Not very well," Finias said. "It not only affects breathing but also limits the amount of oxygen you get into your bloodstream."

"So, it slowly kills you," Cat said, meeting Finias' eyes.

He nodded slowly. "Yes, that's the way poison works," he replied evenly.

"This wasn't poison," Cat argued. "This was darkness. This was evil."

Finias shook his head. "Doesn't matter what you call it, it was poison," he said. "And Donovan allowed it into his system."

"But we got it out, right?" Hazel asked. "He's all fixed up now."

"No, he's not," Henry said, lifting his hands from Donovan and wiping the sweat from his forehead. "We repaired the physical damage, but there's a far more insidious poison lurking inside of Donovan."

"Where?" Hazel asked.

"In his soul," Finias answered. "That's where the demon has its greatest hold on Donovan. That's where the real danger is. All we did this evening is useless if Donovan can't fight off the hold it has on his soul."

"We can't help him?" Cat asked.

Finias shook his head. "I wish we could," he replied sadly. "But this is his war to wage."

"So, what do we do?" Cat asked. "We can't let him just go back out there and be hurt again."

"That depends on what he wants to do," Finias said. "Donovan, can you hear us?"

Donovan nodded slowly and blinked several times before he opened his eyes and looked around the room. He breathed in slowly and then smiled tiredly. "I feel much better," he said. "Thank you. All of you."

174

"The question on the table is, what do we do with you now?" Finias asked.

Donovan tried to sit up, but the iron bands held him in place. He looked at the bands, then up at Finias and sighed. "Okay, so you can't trust me, I get that," he said.

"You can't trust yourself," Finias corrected him. "Or do you remember pointing a gun at me and shooting?"

"The last thing I remember is thinking that I needed to take a break and get some dinner," Donovan replied. "And I think I remember leaving my office, but after that it gets fuzzy."

"Do you remember picking up the gun?" Joseph asked. "Hell, do you even have a license to carry?"

Donovan shook his head. "No to both," he said. "I don't own a gun, with magic I never thought I'd need one and I'm not crazy about iron or steel."

"And yet you had one tonight," Finias said. "Do you remember who gave it to you?"

"No," he replied with frustration. "No, I don't."

"So, you are wondering if we can trust you," Finias stated, his eyebrows lifting in question. "Do you trust yourself?"

Donovan sighed. "No. No, I don't," he said. "But I don't think I can stay locked up forever."

Hazel shrugged. "Maybe just until the Samhain," she suggested.

"No!" Donovan exclaimed vehemently. "No, I need to be able to help."

"Help who?" Finias asked.

"Ellis, that's not fair," Cat cried.

"No. No, he's right," Donovan inserted. "Even with my best intentions, I don't know how much it's controlling me now." He looked over at Finias. "So, you seem to be the guy with all the answers. What's my next step?"

"You need to keep yourself out of its influence until you can regain control of your subconscious," Finias said. "He's got a strong hold on you."

"How long?" Donovan asked.

Finias shook his head. "It all depends on you," he replied. "But for now, let's start with overnight and tomorrow."

"Okay, where am I staying?" Donovan asked.

"I reserved the entire second floor of this bed and breakfast, so you can use the next room," he said. "There are twin beds in there. I'll take the other bed."

"No, I'll take the other bed," Cat said.

Finias turned and studied her for a long moment. "Why?" he asked.

"Donovan put himself in danger for my family…" she began.

"So he says," Finias interrupted.

Cat nodded. "Yes, so he says," she agreed. "But if he's willing to try and break the connection, I have to believe that he was truthful."

"Misguided, but truthful," Joseph added. "An idiot, but truthful. Naïve, but…"

"Yeah, we all get your point," Donovan said to Joseph. "But, Cat, no, I don't want you staying here. I don't remember what I said to you about drinking your blood. But, if there's a chance that I could say something like that again or do something that would harm you, I don't want you anywhere around me."

Finias folded his arms and nodded slowly as he considered the situation. "So, you care about what happens to Cat?" he asked Donovan.

"Yes, I do," Donovan said. "And I won't have her…"

"She's staying," Finias said.

"No!" Donovan exclaimed.

"The person you care about the most is the one who is going to have the greatest chance of saving you," Finias replied. "If she is willing to take the risk, I think she should stay."

"Settled," Cat said.

"Yeah, not quite," Hazel replied. "Let me call Mom and see what she thinks."

Hazel pulled her phone out of her pocket and stared at the screen.

"Dammit," she exclaimed. "Something's happened."

"To your mother?" Finias asked urgently. "What? What's wrong?"

"She was paid a visit by the demon," Hazel replied, reading the text. "He had taken the form of a raven. It got a little dicey until she used the super-soaker filled with holy water. He left quickly after that."

"He's getting stronger," Henry said. "If he's able to either possess animals or shape-shift, his power is growing."

"All the more reason for us to keep Donovan out of his influence," Cat said. "I'll drive back home and get some things for my stay." She turned to her sisters. "And I'll talk to Mom. Okay?"

"Okay," Hazel agreed and then she turned to Finias. "You promise to keep her safe?"

He smiled at Hazel and nodded. "You have my word of honor," he assured her.

Chapter Thirty-one

"No," Agnes said, trying to keep her voice calm and steady as she kept herself busy wiping down a kitchen counter that didn't need cleaning. "And that's the end of it."

"You can't say no," Cat argued. "I'm thirty years old."

"And yet, I did say no," Agnes replied with a shrug. "So, I guess your age doesn't matter, does it?"

"Be reasonable," Cat pleaded.

Agnes clutched the damp rag in her hand and tried to count to ten, but it was no use. She whipped the dishcloth across the room, sending it flying into the sink and, with eyes blazing, turned to her daughter. "Are you kidding me?" she cried. "Be reasonable! What the hell is reasonable about anything that is going on in our lives right now? What the hell is reasonable about you wanting to nurse a man who just threatened to drink your blood? What is reasonable about a crow threatening to kill my family? What is reasonable about anything we are doing right now?"

Agnes felt the angry tears flow down her cheeks, but she didn't bother to wipe them away. "This is not what I thought would happen," she confessed, her voice shaking. "I don't know what I pictured, but not this."

Cat walked across the room and put her arms around her mother, hugging her, offering her comfort. "I don't think any of us pictured this," she said softly. "I always thought it would be like something out of a Disney movie where we all just sing a magic song and wave our wands."

A surprised laugh burbled up from Agnes' throat, and she stepped away from her daughter, wiping away the tears. "I like that version of it," she said, then she sighed. "I'm frightened. Not for myself, but for you and Rowan and Hazel. I'm so frightened for you."

"The thing is, Mom," Cat said. "We're a little freaked out too, but we're not frightened. We're pumped. We're ready. And we're confident that we can do this.

We're confident because you taught us that we could do anything we set our minds on."

Agnes pulled a tissue out of the holder and blew her nose. "So, all of this is my fault," she asked with a sad smile.

"Yeah, if you weren't such a great mom, we would have given up long before this," Cat replied with a sympathetic smile, then she put her hands on her mother's shoulders. "You need to have faith in us. In all you taught us. In the people we are, and the strength we have."

Agnes looked up at her tall daughter and sighed. "Those are the words a mother is supposed to share with her children, not the other way around."

Cat shrugged. "Oh, you probably did," she admitted. "Where else would I learn them?"

"Why do you need to stay with Donovan?" Agnes asked, meeting her daughter's eyes. "Why you?"

That was a fair question, Cat thought. And one that she needed to answer aloud, so she could understand the need herself. Cat stepped away from her mother and

182

took a moment to gather her thoughts. She slipped onto a stool next to the kitchen counter, put her head in her hands, and tried to put those thoughts into words.

"Ellis believes that my connection to Donovan might be just what he needs to overcome the influence of the…" she paused, and Agnes nodded.

"Yes, I know who you're talking about," Agnes inserted, slipping onto the stool next to Cat. "But what if your connection isn't strong enough. What risk do you put yourself in by being there?"

"I don't know," Cat replied frankly, turning toward her mother. "Donovan is bound with iron, so he can't use his powers against me, but I don't know what other things he might be able to manifest with the evil influence inside of him."

"Do you think he has powers beyond witchcraft?" Agnes asked, surprised.

"Well, Ellis said that what happened in the ambulance was because the demon was able to use Donovan as a conduit," Cat explained. "But Ellis has placed wards and charms inside the B&B to keep the demon out."

"Who is this Ellis?" Agnes asked. "And how did he suddenly arrive on the scene and seem to know what's happening?"

Cat shrugged. "Joseph was the first one to meet him," she said. "It sounds like he questioned him and felt good enough about his answers that he let us meet him." She paused for a moment, then added. "And I'm nearly positive that the gun in Donovan's hands was aimed at Ellis and not me. So, he must be a threat to the demon."

"Well, that immediately gives him more points in my book," Agnes replied. "And, before Donovan came in, how was your evening going?"

Cat smiled at her mother. "He's a nice man," she said. "Older, like your age."

"That is not older," Agnes responded immediately. "Why I'm barely middle-aged."

Cat chuckled, and it felt good. "I did feel a friendship, a connection, with him," she said. "But it wasn't romantic at all. It was more trusting or familiar. I don't know, that doesn't make sense, does it?"

Agnes placed her hand on Cat's hand. "Of course, it makes sense," she said. "We can have connections with people we hadn't met in this life because, perhaps, we met them before we were born."

"That's kind of what I feel," Cat said slowly. "That he's familiar but in an otherworldly kind of way."

"But you trust him?" Agnes asked.

Cat nodded. "Yes, I do," she said.

"Did you look?"

Cat's eyes widened in shock. "Mom! Of course, I didn't look," she said. "That would be…"

"Just like what you did with Henry," Agnes reminded her quickly.

Cat shrugged. "Well, yes, but that was different," she hedged.

"Because it was for Rowan, not you, right?" Agnes asked.

Cat grinned. "Exactly," she replied. "So, I'm going back to stay with Donovan?"

Agnes sighed and nodded. "I suppose so," she agreed. "But please be careful."

"I will," she said, kissing her mother's cheek. "I promise."

Chapter Thirty-two

Hazel picked up a deep-fried cheese curd and dipped it in ranch dressing before she took a bite of the oozing, cheesy deliciousness. She sighed in pleasure and leaned back in the patio chair on their back deck. "I think getting take-out from Second Salem was a brilliant idea," she said.

"It was your idea," Rowan replied, munching on a French fry.

"And won't the waitress be surprised when she discovers the food ordered by someone else just disappeared from the kitchen?" Henry asked.

"Well, I paid for it all," Hazel said, justifying her magic as she picked up one more cheese curd. "And I left her a really good tip. All in all, this was a good day."

Joseph, sitting next to her, glanced down and shook his head. "What are you talking about?" he asked. "Donovan nearly killed one of us. A demon attacked him. Cat doesn't know whether or not she can trust him. We have a stranger in town who seems to be all-knowing and a little bit intimidating. And you just ate the last cheese curd."

She looked up at him and grinned. "You snooze, you lose," she replied. "And, to counter your comments. No one got killed. We healed Donovan as much as we could. The demon is barred from Donovan's room, so he has a chance to recover. Mom super-soaked the demon with holy water. And I think Ellis arrived just in time to help us."

"And Cat?" Rowan asked, sipping on her soft drink.

Hazel sighed. "Yeah, well, she probably just talked Mom into letting her go back to Ellis' and stay with Donovan."

Henry shook his head. "There is no way that your mother is going to allow Cat to go back there tonight," he said decidedly. "Absolutely no way."

Hazel looked over at him. "You want to bet?" she asked.

"You've got to be kidding," Joseph exclaimed. "There's way too much danger for her to…"

Joseph's words died in his throat as Cat walked out of the house, a small overnight case in her hand.

"Don't tell me that you think you're going back to the B&B?" Joseph said, standing up and moving in front of Cat.

She looked up at him and nodded. "I don't only think it, I know it," she said firmly.

"No," Joseph said.

Henry stood up and moved into place next to Joseph. "Cat, I'm afraid I have to agree with Joseph," he said. "It's not a good idea for you to put yourself in that kind of danger. You need to stay at home."

She looked from one man to the other and sighed. "You are both really adorable doing the whole big-brother thing," she said. "But I'm going, and you can't stop me."

"Well, no," Henry said. "We could stop you." He glanced over at Rowan. "And your sister will back me up."

Rowan slowly pushed her chair away from the glass-topped table and stood up. Then she sighed and walked across the porch, positioning herself next to her sister. "No, sorry," she said. "I'm backing Cat on this one."

Hazel pushed herself out of her chair and moved to Cat's other side. "Yeah, me too," she said. "Although I agree with Cat. You guys are really sweet."

"Sweet has nothing to do with it," Joseph growled. "This is dangerous. Cat could get hurt, she could get killed."

Hazel nodded. "But she could also save him," she replied softly, meeting Joseph's eyes. "I know how that feels, risking your life for the person you love."

Joseph closed his eyes in frustration and shook his head. Finally, he looked at Hazel, begging for understanding. "But it's not the same," he tried weakly.

She chuckled sadly and stepped forward to kiss him tenderly. "Nice try, big guy," she whispered. Then she turned to Cat. "What can we do to help?"

"Some of that demon-out salve would be awesome," she teased, then she hugged her sisters. "I promise that I'll send out an SOS if anything happens."

"Wait a minute," Henry said, turning and walking towards the stairs. "I just want to grab a few things from my apartment."

"What?" all three sisters asked.

Henry paused half-way down the steps and looked back over his shoulder. "I'm going with you," he said.

"I didn't invite you," Cat replied.

Henry smiled and shrugged. "No, I guess you didn't," he said, hurrying down the steps and jogging across the yard toward the barn.

"He's going anyway, I guess," Rowan said, biting back a smile.

Cat turned to Rowan. "You think this is funny, don't you?" she asked.

"No," Rowan sighed. "I think it's sweet and caring and quite lovely. Isn't he just…"

"A pain in the arse," Cat replied.

"I'll get my things once we get into town," Joseph said. "And I'll follow you and Henry in your car."

"Wait! What?" Cat asked. "When did this turn into a sleepover?"

Joseph grinned at Cat. "Um, just now."

"Should we come too?" Hazel asked.

Cat shook her head. "No, you two need to be here with Mom," she insisted. "In case the demon tries again."

Rowan nodded. "You're right," she said. "But I have to admit that I'll sleep easier knowing you have reinforcements right there with you."

"I have reinforcements," Cat said with frustration. "Ellis will be there."

"Yeah, because we've known Ellis for so long," Hazel inserted. "And he's not mysterious or anything at all."

"Ellis is trustworthy," Cat said.

"Have you looked?" Rowan asked.

"No!" Cat exclaimed. "I would never…"

"You did for Henry," Rowan reminded her.

192

"Henry was unconscious," Cat argued.

Hazel shrugged. "I could hit Ellis over the head with something and knock him out," she offered. "It wouldn't hurt…much."

"That's it," Cat roared in frustration. "I'm leaving now!"

She pushed past Joseph and hurried down the steps to her car. Henry ran from the barn with a backpack flung over his back. "Great timing," he called, reaching the passenger side door as she opened the driver's side.

She glared at him, and he choked a little. "Right, good," he muttered. "I'll just hop on in."

She got in, slamming her door, and in a moment, she was pulling down the driveway with Joseph right behind her.

"I really hope they have a nice time," Hazel said, trying to keep from laughing. Then she turned to her sister. "So, do you want me to order dessert?"

Chapter Thirty-three

Finias pulled the bedroom door closed behind him. Donovan had finally fallen asleep, succumbing to the trauma his body had gone through, and Finias felt it was safe to leave him for a little while. He slipped to the staircase and slowly descended to the first floor. He stopped when he reached the lobby and closed his eyes, allowing his sixth sense to detect the barrier Cat had created in the B&B to hide all the activity on the second floor. He could sense the invisible boundary, moving fluidly between the first and second floors and wrapping itself around the kitchen. He smiled and nodded. "Very well done," he whispered an inflection of pride in his voice.

He moved to the kitchen doorway, where he paused to watch Katie pull a pan of brioche out of the oven. He waited until she safely placed it on the counter before he spoke.

"That looks and smells delicious," he said.

Katie jumped, and her hand flew to her chest. "Oh, my goodness," she exclaimed. "You startled me."

"I apologize," he replied, knowing that normally she would have been able to hear him approach. "I tend to walk very quietly."

She took a deep breath and nodded. "I'll say," she agreed. "You didn't even hit the squeaky floor boards in the dining room." She shook her head dismissively and smiled at him. "What can I do for you?"

"Well, I was only coming down for a couple of herb tea bags," he said. "But the wonderful smells coming from the kitchen drew me in."

Her smile widened. "Well, that is a part of breakfast," she replied, pleased with his compliment. "I'm making French toast with brioche."

"Well, that truly is a decadent breakfast," he said. "I can hardly wait until morning." He nodded his head slightly. "Well, I'm going to just grab those tea bags from the counter in the dining room and get back to my room. Have a nice evening, Katie."

"You too, Ellis," she replied. "And just let me know if there is anything else you need."

His smiled back at her. "Thank you," he said. "You are a very gracious hostess."

He turned and walked out of the kitchen, pausing when he was out of sight, to make sure she returned to her cooking. In a few moments, he could hear the clatter of pans on the counter.

Good, he thought, she doesn't suspect anything.

He hurried to the lobby and stopped at the front door. It was an old oak door with leaded glass in the center. Knowing how old the house was, he quickly inspected the door for signs of protection. Closing his eyes, he used his second sight to locate the markings. He smiled and lifted his hand to touch the faded markings that glowed with light around the leaded window. "Someone has tried to sand you from off the surface of the wood," he said softly. "That's probably how the demon was able to enter."

Pulling a small knife out of his pocket, he reached up and deepened the carved runes around the window and added a few more in inconspicuous spots on the doorframe. He stepped back and closed his eyes once again, viewing them with second sight. The runes glowed brightly with golden-white light. "Better," he whispered. "Much better."

Then he moved to the staircase and sat on the steps, angling his knife to the underside of the banister. With a few quick strokes, he added a few more runes on the underside of the bannister.

That ought to offer a little more protection, he thought.

Then, taking the stairs two at a time, he hurried back to the second floor to prepare for the evening ahead of him and his guest. He had a strong feeling that this was going to be a very interesting night.

Chapter Thirty-four

"I don't want you here," Cat said, her voice clipped as she drove into Whitewater with Henry in the passenger seat.

Henry shrugged easily and glanced over at her set jaw. "Yeah, I can see that," he replied.

She quickly glanced over at him, then returned her focus on the country road ahead of her. "So?" she asked.

"So," he replied slowly, dragging the word out. "I'm sorry, but I couldn't, in good conscience, allow you to go there by yourself."

"Allow me?" she asked, her words clipped.

He sighed. "I didn't mean it that way," he quickly apologized. "What I meant is that we are all in an unusual situation, to say the least. We know, because of my ancestor's grimoire, that we all play a part. Together. So, we need to protect each other, defend each other, and potentially become a nuisance to each other." He stopped and smiled at her. "Because so much depends on all of us making it through this together."

"It's not because I'm a woman?" she asked, still not thawing.

He paused for a long moment, rubbing his hand over his chin as he decided how to answer. "Did you come to the hospital to help me after I'd been shot because I was a man?" he asked.

She quickly glanced over at him again, the surprise registering in her face, and shook her head. "Of course not," she said.

"No, you did it because I was in trouble, and you could help," he replied. "You are one of the most competent people—not women—I know. You have extraordinary abilities, not to mention your raw intelligence. If I were in trouble, you would be one of the first people I'd think to call."

She exhaled slowly, and her hands relaxed on the wheel. "Then why did you insist on coming tonight?" she asked, her voice filled with confusion.

"Because you could be walking into a dangerous situation and I want to be your backup," he said simply.

"Ellis will be…" she began.

"We don't know Ellis," he interrupted. "He might be great, but we don't know that. It's too great a risk…"

"To trust me," Cat finished for him.

"No," he replied adamantly. "To take a chance that our intuition is correct. I like the guy. I actually trust the guy. But we've been fooled before. Hell, Donovan fooled us today. We are too close, the stakes are too high, and the demon wants to win too badly for us to let pride and insecurities break us up."

She glanced over at him again, but this time, there was a flash of humor in her eyes. "No, Henry, why don't you tell me what you really think," she teased.

He chuckled softly. "Perhaps I got a bit carried away just then," he admitted.

She shook her head. "No. No, you didn't," she replied. "You're right. I was a little wrapped up in pride and insecurities." She paused for a moment as a frightening thought came to mind. "Do you think the demon can read our minds?"

"No, I don't," Henry said. "I think he can put thoughts there and make suggestions. But I think rather than reading our minds, he thinks he's an expert on human nature. He believes he knows what makes us tick."

"But you don't think he's got us figured out?" she asked.

Henry shook his head. "No, because he has no concept of love, family, loyalty, and courage," he said softly. "That's his weakness. He thinks we have the same motivations he does, power, control, and hate. And that's why we're going to win."

Cat nodded slowly as she drove past the sign welcoming them to Whitewater. "We have to win," she whispered. "There's no other choice."

"Exactly," Henry agreed. "Which is why we're going to win."

She smiled at him. "I like your attitude, professor," she said.

"Set up the parameters of the outcome before you start," he replied. "And you will achieve the requisite goals and consequences."

"What?" she asked with a soft chuckle.

"Have faith, Cat," he replied. "Just have faith."

Chapter Thirty-five

Agnes poured tea into a delicate bone-china cup and carried it over to the kitchen table where Hazel sat, holding her head in her hands.

"Here, drink this," Agnes encouraged. "It will make you feel better."

Hazel looked up, her face slightly ashen, and nodded. "Thanks," she murmured, taking the cup and sipping the tea. "What the heck is wrong with me? I have a cast-iron stomach."

"Pregnancy will do that to you," Agnes replied sympathetically. "Pregnancy and a dozen deep-fried cheese curds."

Rowan hurried into the room with a small, dark vial in her hand. "Here this is ginger essential oil," she said, unscrewing the lid and placing the opened bottle on the table next to Hazel. "Just breathe it in; it should help with nausea."

Hazel put down her tea cup and picked up the vial, inhaling slowly, closing her eyes as the pungent aroma filled her sinuses. She exhaled slowly, then inhaled again, and felt the queasiness she'd been experiencing dissipate. With a sigh of relief, she put the vial down and picked up the cup. "Better," she breathed, taking another sip of the calming tea. "Much better. Thank you."

Agnes and Rowan sat down on either side of Hazel, relieved to see the color returning to her cheeks. Hazel took another sip of the tea and then shook her head. "This shouldn't be happening to me," she announced.

"What shouldn't?" Agnes asked.

"Sickness," Hazel replied. "That only happens in normal pregnancies."

Rowan put her hand on her sister's arm. "Um, Hazel, this is a normal pregnancy," she explained, biting back a smile.

Hazel shook her head. "No, it's not," she argued. "I mean, we didn't, you know… We didn't…"

Rowan nodded. "Right, you didn't follow the normal biological process of conception, but what you had was more like in vitro fertilization, combined with magic," she explained. "Even though your body was in flex, for lack of a better term, it was still all there, just particulated."

"Like beam me up, Scotty?" Agnes asked.

Rowan smiled. "Exactly," she said, then she turned to Hazel. "And those particulates helped us mesh your DNA to Joseph's, to combat his genetic disease."

"And here's where you get to the part where you and Henry were a little loose with your magic," Hazel said, placing a hand over the slight swell of her abdomen.

"Yeah, well, of course, this is the one time in your life where you actually listen to what I told you to do," Rowan countered. "So, when the spell asked for two to become one so life could be renewed…"

Hazel nodded. "Yeah, we all know what happened next," she interrupted. "Surprise!"

Agnes studied her daughters for a moment and then shook her head. "No, not a surprise," she finally said. "A fulfillment."

"What?" both Hazel and Rowan asked.

"Remember when we read the letter from the grimoire, and it mentioned the three, but parenthetically added a fourth?" she asked. "That fourth soul, a baby, was meant to be in the circle. That fourth soul is vital to our success."

Hazel placed both hands protectively over her belly. "I am not putting this baby at risk," she stated adamantly. "This child is not a sacrifice."

"Of course not," Agnes replied softly. "This child is a gift, a miracle. But not an accident or a mistake. There is a purpose here that perhaps we don't understand, but we need to accept."

Hazel's eyes filled with moisture, and she met her mother's eyes. "I've always thought this baby was a miracle," she said softly. "A part of our destiny."

Rowan wiped away a stray tear sliding down her cheek and smiled at her sister. "You can thank me any time now," she teased.

Hazel reached over and embraced her sister. "Thank you," she whispered, her voice tight with emotion.

Rowan hugged her sister back and waited for a few moments until she could speak. "I will protect your child with my life," she said softly. "We all will."

Hazel leaned back and met her sister's eyes. "I always knew you would."

Chapter Thirty-six

Cat bit back a chuckle when she saw Ellis' eyes momentarily widen in surprise when he saw that she had two companions with her as she ascended the stairs to the second floor of the Bed and Breakfast. She had to give him credit, he schooled his features into calm composure quickly and added a smile of greeting.

"Well, what a surprise," he said, with just a slight hint of irony.

Joseph shrugged and grinned. "I bet you're just thrilled," he said.

"The more the merrier," Finias replied, stepping back into the hallway as they reached the top of the stairs.

"I do apologize," Henry said. "But we insisted that Cat bring us along." He turned and smiled at her. "Actually, we didn't give her a choice. We came along."

"I hope you don't mind," Cat said apologetically. "They were…"

"Just concerned about you," Finias finished. "No. I don't mind at all. There are three bedrooms on the second floor. The third one has a small sitting room and two twin beds." He looked at Joseph and Henry. "I believe you will be comfortable in that room."

"How close is it to the room Cat and Donovan will be in?" Joseph asked.

Finias smiled. "It's across the hall from that room and down the hall from my room."

"Okay, that works," Joseph replied. He turned to Henry. "Why don't you get settled in to our digs while I run to my apartment and pick up a few things."

Then, without waiting for Henry to respond, he turned and quietly walked down the stairs and out the front door.

"Not much on polite, small talk, is he?" Finias asked.

"He's pretty much a straight-to-the-point kind of guy," Cat replied. "How's Donovan doing?"

"The last I checked he was sleeping comfortably," he said. "But that was about fifteen minutes ago. We could all check on him…"

"If it's alright with you," Cat interrupted. "I'd rather just check on him myself. If I need anything, I'll be sure to let you know."

She nodded to both men, then walked past them to the room she'd been in earlier that night.

"That was rather abrupt," Henry said.

Finias nodded as he watched Cat enter the room and close the door behind herself. "Yes, it was," he agreed slowly. "She won't do anything…"

"Stupid?" Henry asked with a wry smile.

"Well, I was going to say impulsive," Finias replied.

Henry shook her head. "No, Cat seems to be the most level-headed of all the sisters," he said. "And Donovan has hurt her before. She won't be too eager to trust him."

Finias nodded, staring at the closed door. "He hurt her badly," he said without thinking.

Henry started. "How did you know?" he asked.

Finias quickly turned back to Henry. "I gathered from the interplay this evening," he improvised. "I'm pretty good at reading undercurrents."

Henry wasn't convinced, but he nodded in agreement. "And there are quite a few undercurrents where these two are concerned," he said. "Are you interested in her?"

Finias smiled slowly. "And that would matter to you because?" he asked.

Henry straightened himself to his full stature and met Finias' eyes. "Because she and her family not only risked their lives to save me," he said pointedly. "They gave back a part of me that had been hidden for most of my life."

"Witchcraft?" Finias asked.

Henry nodded.

"So, you are a novice?" Finias asked, challenging him.

Henry took a deep breath and narrowed his eyes. "No, but I do seem to have a problem with control," he replied softly. "I nearly killed a man. I would hate for that to happen again."

This time Finias' grin broke out into soft laughter. "Very good, Professor," he said. "You are indeed their champion, at a time when a champion is needed. I can assure you that I wish no harm to befall any of the Willoughby ladies. And, I can assure you that my interest in Cat is not nefarious."

"You don't mind if I don't believe you at first?" Henry replied.

"No," Finias said. "I believe you would be a fool to take me at face value without proof."

"And I am no fool," Henry remarked.

Finias shook his head. "No, I don't believe you are," he replied. He sighed and glanced over his shoulder at his bedroom. "I do hate to be a rude host, but I must retire to my room in order to make an important call. Do you mind?"

"No, please," Henry said, motioning towards Finias' room. "I'll just put my things away." He turned, paused, and turned back. "And thank you."

Finias lifted an eyebrow in confusion. "For what?"

"For your assistance. For your hospitality. And for your willingness to fight on our side," Henry replied.

"Are you so sure I'm on your side?" Finias asked.

Henry studied him for a long moment and then nodded slowly. "I'm just about convinced. Good night, Ellis."

Finias schooled his features once again to hide the guilt he felt when Henry used his false name. "Good night, Henry," he replied abruptly, then turned to go into his room.

Chapter Thirty-seven

Cat entered the bedroom and, guided by a dim nightlight, made her way past Donovan's bed to the bed on the other side of the room. She placed her overnight case on the floor and then walked back to check on Donovan.

She bent over him and felt her heart lurch. Although his breathing was normal, it still sounded a little strained, as if every breath was a reminder of the pain he'd been through. His complexion was not as pale, but she could still see dark shadows underneath his eyes and beads of perspiration on his forehead.

Reaching over to the nightstand next to his bed, she picked up a soft cotton washcloth and gently wiped away the moisture.

"Cat," he murmured in his sleep.

"Shhhh, darling," she whispered back, gently pushing his hair off his forehead. "You need to sleep."

He exhaled softly, and she saw some of the tension leave his face. Then his face contorted, and his body shuddered. "Help me," he whispered hoarsely.

She lifted her hand, moving it to connect with him and give him strength, then froze. Doubt, thick and tangible, stopped her. Was he still connected to the demon? Was this another ploy to pull her in, fill her mind with unspeakable horrors?

She stepped backwards, away from the bed, and grasped her hands behind her back. "I can't help you," she replied softly. "You have to make this journey on your own."

"Cat," he begged. "Cat don't leave me."

She shook her head and wiped the tears from her cheeks. "I never left you," she replied. "You left me."

Even in his delirium, her words pushed through and exposed a memory that he had tried to forget.

He was standing in the forest, in front of the shelter on the escarpment above the lake. His duffle bag was packed with all of his earthly possessions, and he had a ticket for the Greyhound bus in his back pocket. And

now, now was the worst part of it all. He had to say good-

bye.

Would she understand? he wondered as he

watched the path that led to the Willoughby home. Would

she know that he was leaving for her?

He sighed and shook his head. No, he needed to

be honest with himself. He was leaving for himself. He

was leaving because someday, when he was a little older,

he wanted to offer Catalpa Willoughby a life with an

honorable, successful man. Not a life with a juvenile

delinquent whose parents abandoned him as soon as they

were able. He didn't want charity. He didn't want

sympathetic looks from the Willoughbys. He wanted them

to look at him with awe in their eyes, with admiration, and

even more important, respect.

He heard the steps in the distance and focused all

of his attention on the path.

The sun was sparkling, catching the red and

brown hues in Cat's hair. Her caramel-colored skin

seemed to glow, and her smile made his heart thump in his chest. He prayed she'd understand. She saw him, and her smiled widened. "Donovan," she cried out, breaking into a run.

She threw herself into his arms and lifted her lips for a kiss. He couldn't deny her a kiss; he couldn't deny himself one last kiss. With slow deliberation, he glided his lips over hers, tasting the sunshine and the warmth. Then he deepened the kiss; exploring, feasting, and anxiously trying to communicate his feelings. She moaned; it was a sound that was both sensual and frightened. She looked up at him, her lips bee-stung and moist. "Donovan?" she asked, and he could hear the concern.

He bent forward and kissed her again, a light, poignant kiss. Then he stepped away.

"I'm leaving, Cat," he said.

She shook her head. "But I just got here," she said. "Can't you stay for a little while longer?"

"No, I don't mean I have to go home," he explained. "I mean, I'm leaving. I'm leaving Whitewater."

217

*He remembered the way she stared at him,
confusion first, then shock, and finally, when his words
sunk in, pain.*

*"No," she replied adamantly. "No, you can't
leave. I love you."*

*Words that should have brought joy, now brought
pain and regret. He believed her. In her own way, Cat
loved him. But he wondered if it was like the love she
would give to any of the strays she and her sisters had
adopted and saved. He didn't, couldn't be another project.
Another Willoughby good deed. He needed to earn her
love and respect.*

"I'm going to school," he replied. "In Chicago."

*She shook her head as her eyes filled with tears.
"No. No, you said you'd go to school here, in
Whitewater," she argued, "until I finish high school."*

*"I got a better deal in Chicago," he replied
coolly, desperate to keep any emotion out of his voice.
"It's just the way it is."*

Her head shot up as if she'd been slapped. The sorrow in her eyes was replaced with anger and pain. "That's just the way it is?" she asked, her voice filled with rage.

The trees around them shuddered, and the sky filled with dark clouds. Thunder rumbled in the distance. "That's just the way it is?" she repeated, the wind whipping around her, stirring up dust and debris like a maelstrom. She began to lift her hands in preparation for a spell.

Donovan took a deep breath and met her eyes. "Remember, an harm it none, Cat," he reminded her. "But I understand if you feel the need to hurt me. I guess I deserve it. So, you have my permission to do what you need to do."

Her hands dropped to her sides, and the winds died down immediately. Tears streamed down her face as she looked at him. "Why, Donovan? Why?" she whispered hoarsely.

He took a deep breath and pushed back his own tears. "Because it's something that I need to do," he replied.

He reached back into the shelter, lifted his duffle bag, and hefted it over his shoulder. Without looking back, he walked down the trail toward town. He heard the sound of her knees hitting the soft ground. Heard the pain in her muffled anguished cries. And felt the pain of her breaking heart as it echoed in his own.

Chapter Thirty-eight

Standing only a few feet from his bed, Catalpa watched the expressions change on Donovan's face as he slept and wondered about his dreams. At least the stark look of pain was gone, but it was now replaced by a deep sadness that made her heart ache for him. She brushed away the remaining tears and shook her head resolutely. "Don't get pulled in again," she warned herself softly. "Last time, it was only a broken heart. This time it could be the death of my family."

Backing away from him, she moved to the bed on the other side of the room. She took a deep breath, trying to remove all of the negative emotions that had built up that day, but the melancholy hung over her like a raincloud.

"This is so not working," she whispered with frustration. "Okay, Cat, it's time to take charge."

Pulling off her shoes and tossing them to the side, she climbed onto the bed and sat, her back against the wall, legs folded into a Lotus position and hands resting limply against her knees. She took another, slower, breath, and finally closed her eyes. She whispered the age-old mantra and felt her mind clear, like the sun bursting through clouds on a rainy day. She saw him in the distance and felt a surge of relief course through her body. He would know. He would understand. She moved to the shadowy figure and rested near his side. Although she had never been able to discern any visual details, the bulk of his shadow was comforting and welcoming.

"I've been waiting to hear from you," her spirit guide chastised lightly. "How was your date?"

Cat smiled. "Well, the good news is I didn't die," she began.

"You didn't…" he gasped, and then he took a deep breath. "Perhaps you should explain."

Her smile widened. It felt good to be able to talk to someone who truly understood her. She leaned back against the bedroom wall and relaxed, her eyes still closed, and continued to converse with her spirit guide.

She told him about the events of the evening, only pausing when she came to the part where Donovan grabbed her arm in the ambulance.

"What happened next?" he asked softly.

She sighed. "Donovan grabbed my arm and told me that he was going to drink my blood," she said, surprised at the strength of her voice and the lack of fear she felt when she repeated the words. "Then he said he was going to burn my body as a sacrifice."

The spirit guide was quiet for a moment and finally spoke. "Did you realize this was not your friend speaking, but the one who would control him?" he asked.

"Well, actually, a friend told me that it wasn't Donovan," she admitted thoughtfully. "I have to admit, because of the earlier vision…"

"Ah, yes," the spirit guide replied. "The one we were going to face together. Isn't it interesting that the demon chose to use that choice of words from Donovan's mouth?"

Cat's mouth dropped. "He knew," she whispered as understanding dawned. "He knew what would frighten me. He knew I'd seen the earlier vision. It really wasn't Donovan."

"No, it wasn't Donovan," the spirit guide replied. "But, unfortunately, your friend has chosen the wrong associates."

Shaking her head, Cat made a startling discovery. "He didn't choose them for himself," she said slowly. "He chose them because he thought that by being in their camp, he could protect us."

"Are you sure?" the spirit guide asked.

She nodded slowly, but with emerging certainty. "Yes, I am sure," she whispered.

"Is that certainty based on logic and common sense, or some other emotion?" he asked.

"Are you asking me if I am still in love with him?" she responded. "And if that love could somehow blind me to his failings?"

"No," he replied kindly. "But I believe you are asking yourself those questions."

She exhaled slowly. "This is some kind of psychotherapy, isn't it?" she asked. "When I want an answer from you, you just reply 'What do you think?'"

He chuckled softly. "What do you think?" he replied, half kindly, half ironically.

"I think you know exactly what I think," she replied with a frustrating huff.

"That's neither here nor there," he said. "You need to decide, for yourself, if Donovan is a man you can trust, not only with your life, but with the lives of your family."

"That's not easy," she immediately answered.

"Actually, it is," he said. "It comes down to if you trust him or not. Trust, like integrity, is one of those characteristics that are all or nothing."

But what if I trust him again and he hurts me again?" she asked quietly, the pain tangible in her voice.

"He can only hurt you if you allow him to," he replied.

She shook her head in confusion. "So, I shouldn't let him into my heart?" she asked.

"No, I didn't say that, little one," he replied.

"I'm confused," she said.

She could feel the warmth and love coming from him, directed towards her. "Do you remember when you were a child, and we would talk about butterflies?" he asked.

She nodded, and a soft smile lit upon her lips. "About how I needed just to open my hand and allow them to rest there, but not try to catch them?"

"Exactly so," he said. "Because catching them…" He paused.

"Would only kill them and disappoint me," she answered.

"You took pleasure in what they were willing to give you," he reminded her. "They delighted you by resting on your hand, displaying their vibrant colors, and then flying away to continue their journey."

"Yes," she said. "But what does that have to do…"

"You didn't get hurt because they left, did you?" he interrupted.

"No," she said.

"Why not?"

"Because they were supposed to leave," she replied. "I didn't expect them to stay. I could enjoy them for that short time I had them on my hand."

"And why is that any different than trusting Donovan for what he can give you?" he asked. "If you don't expect him to stay, to love you, then you won't be disappointed…"

"I won't be hurt," she inserted. "He didn't hurt me; my expectations of what I wanted to happen hurt me."

"You were always very clever," he remarked.

"But how can I keep myself from loving him?" she asked.

"You can't," he said sadly. "But you can understand that loving someone doesn't necessarily guarantee a return of that emotion. As long as you can love and let him go…"

"I won't be disappointed," she said.

"You will be sad when he leaves," he counseled. "But the sad will not be encased in bitterness."

She lifted a hand and wiped a tear that slowly stole its way down her cheek. "I can do that," she said, nodding. "I can let him go."

"Then, perhaps, you can also trust him," he suggested.

"Yes," she said, her voice filled with determination. "Yes, I can."

"Catalpa," he said gently. "He may surprise you and return your love."

She took a deep, shuddering breath. "And he may not," she replied sadly. "But our focus needs to be on defeating the…"

"Catalpa!" he cut her off before she could mention the demon's name.

"Oh," she exclaimed, covering her mouth with her hands. "Oh, I'm sorry."

"No, you are tired," he replied gently. "And you need to sleep, not worry. I will be close tonight, watching over you. Sleep."

"But I need to…," she began, then stopped to yawn widely. "I need to…"

"Rest, sweet Catalpa," he soothed. "Lie down on the bed and rest."

Suddenly overwhelmed by exhaustion, Cat stretched out onto the bed, burrowing her head into the softness of the pillow and in moments she was breathing slowly, sound asleep.

She slammed the door to her bedroom and threw herself onto the bed. This time it had been worse. This time she'd had to stand alone against the members of the coven as they called her cruel names and made her feel like she was more of an outsider than she already felt.

Her sisters hadn't been the target, perhaps because they were younger. Or perhaps because their coloring fit in more with the other students in Whitewater. And this time there had been no Donovan to walk slowly to her side and intimidate the others into leaving her alone.

They knew he'd left. They knew she'd lost not only her protector, but her soul mate. They told her that he'd found other, prettier girls. They told her that he'd called them, laughed with them about the stupid crush she had on him. Told them about her inexperience and ignorance. Told them that he was glad to be out of Whitewater and far away from Catalpa Willoughby.

Hot tears fell on her pillow as she wept and then, finally exhausted, she fell into a deep sleep.

"Cat, I will always love you."

She could hear his voice in her dreams. She could feel his hand tenderly wipe away the tears. She could feel the butterfly-light touch of his lips on her forehead.

230

"Be strong, for just a little longer," he had pleaded. "I'll come back to you a better man. I promise I'll come back to you."

But, of course, when she woke up, he wasn't there. How many times had she dreamed the same dream? How many times, when she was near waking, she could almost feel his presence in her room? How many times had she been buoyed up, only to be let down when she opened her eyes and found that she was still alone?

How many times would she believe that he still cared?

Chapter Thirty-nine

Catalpa's slow and steady breathing mirrored Donovan's in the otherwise silent room. The light from the table lamp shone dimly and only illuminated the room slightly, casting pale shadows on the wooden floor. For a moment, the room was at peace, as were the two occupants, dreaming of simpler times and places, forgetting the horrors of the day.

But, it seemed, one horror would not give up so easily.

In the corner of the room, the space between the tall, narrow closet door and the wooden planked floor was suddenly illuminated with a muted, red glow. Almost immediately after the appearance of the glow, the cast-iron doorknob on the closet door stirred, angling to one side and then the other. It moved slowly, deliberately, but cautiously, so nothing would awaken the dreamers.

Finally, the latch slipped out of its slot, and the door slowly opened. The light disappeared and, in its

232

place, a shadow slipped from the confines of the closet, pouring darkness into the dimly lit room. The darkness pooled on the floor, then oozed and bubbled like liquid tar as it rolled silently towards Donovan's bed. Reaching the side of the bed, the shadow began to transform into a solid being, stretching up and looming over the sleeping man. As the transformation finished, the planes and curves of something resembling a face moved into place. The chin was narrow and long, the nose flat and wide, the cheekbones stark and pointed, and then suddenly gleaming red eyes blazed out from newly created eye sockets and cast a hue on Donovan's face.

Donovan stirred in his sleep, tossing his head restlessly as if he could sense the darkness next to him. He moved his arms, and the handcuffs rattled in response. In unconscious frustration, he yanked on the cuffs again, trying to get away from the disturbing feelings.

A low growl came from the inside of the shadow, and then it bent, slowly encapsulating Donovan's arms in its depths. A moment later, a muted clang sounded, and the handcuffs fell away from Donovan's wrists. The shadow moved to the end of the bed, and the leg cuffs opened in the same manner.

"Donovan," his name was whispered urgently inside his head. "Donovan, awake!"

Waking from a deep sleep, Donovan slowly opened his eyes to the darkness surrounding him. "Where…" he started to murmur, but before he could finish his words, the shadow loomed over him. Slowly the darkness enveloped him, moved through his skin, and sunk into his body.

Donovan shuddered, then sat up and took a deep, satisfying breath. He looked down at his unencumbered wrists and flexed them with pleasure. "Much better," he whispered, his voice mirroring the voice that had just ordered him to awaken.

Then he turned his head and looked across the room at Cat, sound asleep on her bed. His eyes glowed red, and his smile widened. "Much, much better," he whispered and then he slowly licked his lips. "I'm going to enjoy this very much."

Donovan was inside a nightmare, trapped inside of a body that had been taken over by something else. He looked down at his hands and saw that the handcuffs were gone, but when he saw his hands flexing without his direction, the panic turned to terror. He watched, through the red hue of his vision, his focus turn toward Cat and heard the demon's delight.

"No!" he screamed internally. "No! You will not touch her!"

Mocking laughter greeted his plea. "We'll both touch her," the voice inside his head taunted.

Donovan tried to stop his body from moving, but he watched in horror as his legs slid off the bed and slowly moved across the room.

"No!" he screamed again, his alarm echoing in his brain. "No, you can't do this!"

"Oh, I can do anything I want to," the demon responded. "You invited me in, and now your body is under my control."

Donovan's body stumbled, the demon not used to being inside a flesh and blood entity, and his movements were slow. But Donovan could see that they would be beside Cat's bed in just a few more slow steps.

He has my body, he thought, but not my mind.

Fighting through the fear, Donovan concentrated on linking with Cat. He pushed through her sleepy haze and connected with her thoughts. "Run!" he screamed. "Cat, run! The demon has control over me! Run!"

Cat's eyes opened, and she stared at Donovan in confusion.

"Donovan?" she stammered as she shook her head.

"Cat, darling," the demon murmured. "I'm in so much pain, help me."

"RUN!" Donovan screamed into her thoughts.

Eyes widened in shock, she crawled to the back of the bed and slid away from him. "Leave him," she commanded.

The demon laughed harshly and waved Donovan's arm to the side, moving a dresser across the room to bar the door. "Not until I've enjoyed myself with you," he replied.

Cat tasted fear as she remembered the image she'd seen in Donovan's mind, then she immediately remembered what her spirit guide had told her. The demon had used that to create fear. He was playing with her. He was manipulating her.

Fear turned to anger, and she faced him.

"Go to hell," she raged.

She took a deep breath, waved her arms, and recited the spell.

Seal and cover every break,

From this room, the air I take,

And send it far away from me,

As I wish, so mote it be.

237

Suddenly a small, lavender cyclone appeared in the center of the room. It rotated quickly, pulling the air from all corners of the room and sending it up through a darker, purple swirling vortex and out of the room. Blankets, pillows, and sheets danced around the room, caught in the powerful winds. Lamps toppled, pictures were pulled from the walls, and knickknacks flew from dresser tops and shelves, joining the swirling gales.

Donovan gasped as the air in the room diminished and struggled to stay upright. In his already weakened condition, his vision began to darken almost immediately, and he could feel the demon's power diminish as his body began to lose consciousness.

I'm dying, he thought, Cat's only escape was to kill me.

He teetered on the edge of darkness and reached out to her mind once more. "Cat," he whispered. "I will always love you."

Then everything went dark.

Chapter Forty

As soon as Donovan hit the floor, Cat stopped the cyclone, and the door burst open, the powerful thrust shoving the dresser violently to the side. Ignoring the door, Cat hurriedly knelt at Donovan's side and placed her hand on his neck, relieved to find a weak, but steady pulse.

"What the hell do you think you're doing?" Henry asked, climbing over the debris scattered around the room from the cyclone's winds.

Gasping for breath, Cat held up her hand, asking Henry to give her a moment, while she caught her breath. She bent over, her hands on her knees, while she drank in huge gulps of air. Finally, she straightened and turned to Henry. "Somehow the demon was able to enter the room and Donovan," she said.

"And Donovan what?" Henry asked as he walked around the room, examining the area.

"The demon was able to enter Donovan," she clarified. "He took over Donovan's body."

"But, that's impossible," Finias said from the doorway. "I put wards throughout the house. There's no way he could have entered."

Cat shrugged. "Well, something didn't work," she replied. "Because if Donovan hadn't warned me…" She shuddered as she thought about the vision she'd seen.

"Wait, he warned you?" Finias asked, as he too stepped over the overturned furniture strewn across the floor and made his way to Cat. "How did he do that if the demon was controlling him?"

"He reached out and connected with me through his mind," she replied. "We used to do it all the time when we were…"

She paused, looked down at the unconscious man next to her, and sighed. "A long time ago," she finished softly.

"That would take a very strong link," Finias said, kneeling next to her and Donovan. "A remarkably strong link. He saved your life."

She nodded. "I know," she agreed.

Finias placed his hand on Donovan's shoulder and closed his eyes. "I can't feel another presence in him," he said, then he opened his eyes and looked at Cat. "What did you do?"

"I sucked all of the air out of the room," she said. "I thought if Donovan were unconscious, the demon wouldn't have a whole lot of power."

"Why didn't you pass out too?" Henry asked, from the corner of the room.

She smiled slightly. "I was always the winner at the how-long-can-you-hold-your-breath contests," she said with a slight shrug. "You never know when random skills will come in handy."

Henry turned from Cat to the closet. He held his hand up and whispered a short incantation. Suddenly the

241

closet glowed red. "It came through here," he said. "There are still residual traces on the floor and the doorknob."

Finias stood up and walked over to Henry, examining the space. "I don't understand how it could enter," he said, mystified. "I thought I blocked every entrance."

Henry leaned back against the wall and nodded slowly. "Maybe he isn't entering the house," he said slowly. "Maybe he's part of the house."

"What?" Cat asked.

"I've been doing quite a bit of research on the Spiritualism Movement in the United States, and I found that one of the more popular spells during the spiritualism revival was a binding spell," Henry explained. "Generally, it was used in a positive manner, like a binding spell to ensure a happy marriage. But there were cases when something was bound to a place."

"Like they were imprisoned in it?" Cat asked.

Henry nodded. "If they did it correctly," he said. "But, if they didn't do it right, then the house could be bound to the demon and not the other way around."

"Giving him easy access to the house because it becomes part of him," Finias inserted. "Which explains how he by-passed the wards and charms."

"But how can we know for sure?" Cat said.

"We need to find the records of the group that accidentally summoned him in the first place," Henry said. "And see if they tried to undo their mistake by binding him."

"What the hell did you do to Donovan?"

Cat, Henry, and Finias turned to see Joseph standing in the doorway of the room.

"It's a long story," Cat said. "But even more pressing, what are we going to do with him now?"

Chapter Forty-one

"Well, it's obvious he's not safe here," Finias said, gazing around the destroyed room. "And he's not going to stay unconscious for much longer."

Joseph picked his way across the room, carefully stepping over the debris, and knelt next to the unconscious man. "Well, he's not safe in his apartment or his offices," he said. "I hid cameras in both spots to track what he was doing."

"You did what?" Cat exclaimed.

Joseph turned to her and shrugged. "He was acting weird, and I was worried," he said. "And with the deadline of Samhain closing in, I didn't want to waste any time."

She sighed and nodded in understanding. "So, what did you find?" she asked, her stomach clenching with concern.

"It's not him," Joseph said. "He's not into evil and power, but he's being unconsciously influenced by it."

"I don't understand how that can happen," Henry said. "Evil just can't take us over; we have to let it in at some point."

"Well, yeah, he did," Joseph said. "At the last ceremony, when they were trying to kill Hazel. Donovan thought he could be a spy; pretend he was with them and then help us. But that's not how it works. Once you let them in a little, they take a lot more than you realize."

"What did your cameras show?" Finias asked.

"I saw Donovan doing a lot of things when he was in a semi-conscious state," Joseph replied. "Almost like he was sleep-walking. And tonight, when he got the gun, he wasn't even looking at the desk drawer when he pulled it out and stuffed it into his waistband. It was like something else was controlling him."

"Well, something else was," Cat said. "Just like tonight."

"Okay, so we go back to the initial question, where do we take him, and how do we get him there?" Henry asked.

"Rowan has some herbs that can cause a trance-like state," Henry suggested. "We could give him those and move him to Willoughby house."

"So, drug him," Joseph inserted, then he turned to Finias. "You seem to have more experience in these kinds of things. If we drug Donovan, does that make his body incapable of possession?"

Finias shook his head. "No, I'm afraid not," he replied. "As you mentioned, you caught Donovan in a trance-like state doing things for the demon. If the demon gets in his body, he can control it, even if Donovan is sound asleep."

"And since the demon has been in there at least once before," Cat added. "It's easier for him to get in there again."

"So, we change him into something, that even if possessed, is harmless," Henry suggested.

"Like what?" Cat asked skeptically.

Henry shrugged. "A mouse or a hamster," he suggested.

"If Fuzzy didn't eat him, then Esmerelda certainly would," Cat replied, referring to their wolf and their cat. "It's got to be something a little bigger than that."

"A puppy," Finias said. "Although he could still bite, he could be more easily controlled, and he wouldn't be in danger of being devoured by your wolf."

Cat paused and stared at Finias. "How did you know that we had a wolf?" she asked.

Finias momentarily froze, then he smiled and shrugged. "You must have told me about him," he said easily. "How else could I have known?"

"How else indeed," Joseph muttered softly, and Henry sent him a startled look.

But Cat, missing Joseph's comment and Henry's surprise, just nodded and smiled. "Things have been so crazy in these past few hours, I suppose I don't know what I've said," she confessed.

"I agree a puppy would work," Henry added. "Especially if we put him in a crate to confine him while you drove home."

"Me? Drive home? By myself?" Cat asked, surprised. "I thought that one of you would…"

"Oh, well, if you need one of us to come with you, we certainly will," Joseph inserted.

She shook her head quickly. "No. I mean, no, I guess you don't need to come," she stammered. "I'm sure that I can handle…"

"Yes, that's what we thought too," Henry interrupted. "Especially if he's in a crate."

"Okay, well then, let's get this done, and I'll get home," Cat said. "No sense wasting time."

Chapter Forty-two

The cute, little black Labrador Retriever puppy was still sound asleep when Henry placed it on a blanket inside the doggie crate Hazel had sent over. "He's still crashed out," he said softly, as he locked the carrier door. "But even if he wakes up, he won't be able to get out and cause any trouble."

"Will he still have his powers when he wakes up?" Cat asked as they stowed her overnight case into the back seat of her car.

Henry nodded. "Yes, he will," he explained. "But because he'll be in a puppy body, it'll take him a while to figure out how to use them. By that time, you should be safe and secure behind the walls of your home."

"You're sure the demon is no longer within him?" Cat asked. "I don't want to bring anything inside that could harm my family."

"There's no demon now," Henry said, placing his hand on the puppy's side and checking once more. "But,

249

before you bring the puppy in, why don't you sprinkle some holy water on it. If the demon has snuck in while you were traveling, you'll be able to find out right away."

She nodded. "Good idea," she replied, and then she met his eyes. "You were so concerned about me coming over here on my own tonight. Why aren't you concerned about me traveling back home on my own?"

"Truth?" Henry asked, glancing over his shoulder to make sure they were far enough away from the house that no one could hear them.

"Yes, truth," Cat said firmly.

"There's just something about Ellis that has both Joseph and me concerned," he confessed. "I feel like he's hiding something and I'm not too sure whose side he's really on."

"But he's helped us so much," Cat argued quietly.

Henry nodded slowly. "Could be," he agreed. "But it also could be that he set us up. He told us the demon couldn't enter the room. He told us that you would be safe. He put you in the room with Donovan." He folded his arms across his chest. "Could be that he's just as surprised as we are that the demon got through or, it could be that it was part of his plan. Anyway, we figure having both of us staying close to him will make you and your family safer in the long run. Besides, both Rowan and Hazel will be monitoring your ride home and will be at your side in a moment's notice."

After depositing the puppy and the carrier on the passenger's side seat, Henry opened the driver's door, so Cat could slide in. Once she was seated behind the wheel, he leaned forward, one hand on the roof of the car, the other on the top of the door, and looked down at her. "Now, don't speed and don't run any stop signs," he teased, then his face sobered. "Let us know when you make it home, okay. And don't take any chances. If you feel nervous, let us know, and we'll be there immediately."

She nodded. "I will. I promise," she said, sliding the key into the ignition and turning on the car. "And Henry…"

251

Henry paused before closing the door.

"Be careful," she ordered.

He smiled at her and nodded. "Yes, I will," he said. "You too."

He closed the door firmly, and Cat backed out of the parking spot and drove across the parking lot to the road.

What the hell has happened to me?

The question came directly into Cat's head from the seat next to her. She glanced over, and the puppy was looking at her.

"I'm taking you back to Willoughby Farm," she explained. "That's the only place where the demon doesn't seem to have access to you."

What happened to my body?

Cat grinned. "I think you look adorable," she teased. "And I've always wanted a puppy of my own."

Funny, Cat, now what's going on?

She sighed. "Do you remember what happened in the bedroom?" she asked.

The puppy whined softly and put its head between its paws. *It got to me, didn't it? Somehow the demon got into me and was trying to hurt you.*

She nodded. "It entered you and took you over," she explained. "But somehow you were able to still connect with me and warn me."

The whirlwind, you conjured a whirlwind and sucked the air out of the room. You didn't get hurt?

"No, I'm fine," she said. "But we realized that the demon could get to you at the B&B, so we needed to get you to our house. But I needed to put you in a form that could be controlled in case the demon decided to jump you before we got to the house."

A puppy, really?

She laughed. "A really cute puppy," she said. "Anything smaller might have been too tempting for Fuzzy and Esmeralda. And anything bigger would have been too potentially dangerous for me."

Makes sense. So how long do I have to stay like this?

"Just until we get home and I test you to be sure you're all alone in there," she explained.

The puppy shook its head and sighed. *Maybe you should keep me like this until you can be sure I can be trusted.*

Cat glanced over at him. "I trust you, Donovan," she said softly.

The puppy stood up, wagged its tail and pushed its nose against the bars of the carrier. *Thank you, Cat. You don't know how much that means to me.*

"You're welcome," she said. "But you need to realize you're still vulnerable to its influence."

The puppy nodded and laid down. *Yeah, you're right.*

Then he looked up, cocked his head to one side, and yapped at her. *Well, as long as you're not thinking of taking me to the pound, I think we have a chance.*

Laughing, she reached over to the carrier, slipping her finger inside and stroking the top of the puppy's head.

"I can't," she said sincerely. "I need you, Donovan. We all

need you to stop the demon."

Chapter Forty-three

Finias, Joseph and Henry watched silently as Cat's car drove down the street and finally turned right, heading toward her home. Several moments after the car had disappeared from sight, Finias turned to the other two men. "Do you want to tell me why you felt you needed to stay with me instead of accompanying Cat?" he asked.

Joseph shrugged easily. "Do you want to tell us why you didn't volunteer to accompany Cat to her home?"

"Or how you knew that Cat had a wolf when she didn't mention it?" Henry added.

Finias folded his arms across his chest and nodded slowly. "It would seem that we are at an impasse, gentlemen," he replied. "I can assure you that I mean no harm to any one of the Willoughbys, but I cannot divulge any more than that at this time."

"And we're just supposed to trust you, right?" Joseph asked, shaking his head slowly. "Not going to happen."

"Actually, yes, you are just going to have to trust me," Finias replied, "because you need all the help you can get to defeat this thing."

Henry sighed. "Actually, he's right, we do need all the help we can get," he said to Joseph, then he turned to Finias. "But it would make the entire ordeal much more palatable if you could offer us something that would help us feel more comfortable working with you."

Finias was silent for a few moments, as he contemplated their request, then finally, he nodded. "Okay, I can tell you that I have been Catalpa's spirit guide since she was a child," he confessed. "Which is why I knew about the wolf and other parts of her life. I've always had a long-distance relationship with her. But I was shown a vision several months ago, about Catalpa and her family, and knew that I had to come and help."

"Why didn't you want her to know?" Henry asked.

"She still needs her spirit guide right now," Finias explained. "She needs the anonymous counselor who she's trusted her entire life."

Joseph nodded. "Yeah, I get it," he said. "It's like virtual friends. It's cool when it's just texting or emails, but once you decide to meet face to face, the whole dynamic changes."

"Now that I've shared that with you, can we get to work?" Finias asked.

Henry paused a moment, studied Finias' face, and then continued. "Alright then, Ellis. You mentioned that we needed to do some research to see if any other spells or bindings were performed. There's a Museum of Spiritualism a couple of blocks away, and if there are any records about the Pratt Institute and what they did, it will be there. We just need to go over and look."

"Isn't that breaking and entering?" Finias asked.

Joseph chuckled. "Not when you have the Chief of Police along with you," he said. "I'm sure we saw someone inside the building, and we are just investigating."

Finias smiled and nodded. "What are we waiting for?"

They took Joseph's cruiser because it was more official and, with a quick spell on the aluminum locks, they had the door opened and the alarm silenced in a matter of moments. Finias waved his hand, and the area around them was illuminated, so they didn't need to use flashlights. They slowly looked around the main room, each separating and going in different directions.

Displays and dioramas were lined up on every wall, including a miniature of Whitewater's downtown one hundred years earlier. A life-sized poster of Morris Pratt stood in one corner, staring out into the center of the room. Finias and Joseph met at that point and looked at the aged man in the dark suit.

"Now that's creepy," Joseph said, walking forward and then moving back. "His eyes follow you."

"Are you afraid of ghosts?" Finias asked.

"No," Joseph replied, moving forward and back once again. "Just creeped out by dead old guys."

"I found it," Henry called from across the room.

Finias and Joseph looked over and saw Henry standing next to an open door that led to a smaller room. "This is the research area," Henry said. "There's quite an extensive library inside."

"Leave it to the professor to find the library," Joseph replied wryly.

They hurried over, entered the room, and were met with floor to ceiling bookshelves that covered three walls.

"You weren't kidding about extensive," Joseph said. "Any idea what we're looking for?"

"I think it would be a diary or a notebook of some sort," Henry said. "Probably handwritten. It could even be an essay book, because it was a school."

Joseph nodded. "I'll start over there," he said, pointing to the northeast corner of the room.

"I'll search across from you," Finias offered.

"Okay, I'll start here," Henry said, turning to face the tall stacks before him.

Then he looked back over his shoulders, to the other two men and reminded them, "Search like your life depends on it. Because it does."

Chapter Forty-four

"Oh, he's is so cute!" Hazel cooed as she lifted the carrier from the car. "Look at those adorable ears and those eyes." She looked up over the carrier to meet her sister's eyes. "Can we keep him, please?"

The puppy barked indignantly at Hazel and Cat laughed. "Donovan is not at all amused," she said.

Hazel lifted the carrier higher, so she was nose to nose with the pup. "Oh, is the little, tiny puppy upset with the big witchy lady?" she asked in an indulgent voice. "Well, the big witchy lady is just shaking in her boots."

When the puppy growled and barked again, Hazel laughed delightedly. "We really don't have to turn him back, do we?"

They walked to the back porch and, when Hazel started up the steps, Cat put a hand on her shoulder to stop her. "Wait," she said. "We need to be sure he's still okay."

"But we have wards," Hazel said. "So, the demon couldn't…"

"Unless we invite him in," Agnes said from the top step.

"Right," Hazel said, placing the carrier on the ground. "What do we do?"

"Holy water," Cat said, and she looked up at her mother.

Agnes hurried over to the chair that held the large squirt gun and picked it up. "I never realized how important these would be for our safety," she said, tossing the toy to her daughter.

Cat looked down at the puppy. "Donovan sit," she commanded. The puppy plopped its bottom down immediately and looked up at Cat. "Close your eyes."

"Cat, a puppy's not going to know…" Hazel began, but then she stopped when the puppy obediently closed its eyes.

"It's not a puppy," Cat reminded her sister. "It's Donovan."

Then she aimed the gun and shot the holy water into the carrier, hitting the puppy on the shoulder and the chest. The puppy sat still, its tongue lolling out of its mouth, and its tail wagging back and forth. Cat aimed and shot one more time; the puppy continued to sit, enjoying the splash of water.

"Okay, we're good," she said. "Quickly bring him inside before anything changes."

Hazel scooped the carrier up and ran up the stairs. Cat followed closely behind, carrying the squirt gun and her overnight case. Agnes waited on the top of the stairs for her daughter and hugged her once she stepped onto the porch. "How are you, really?" she asked.

Cat smiled at her mother and nodded. "I'm good," she said. "I feel stronger and surer of myself."

"And Donovan?" Agnes asked.

Cat sighed. "I trust him, Mom," she said. "He wants to help us." Then she shrugged. "And I'm not going to think about anything beyond that right now."

"But, honey, Donovan…" Agnes began, but Cat shook her head.

"No, Mom, nothing beyond the here and now. We all just need to concentrate on the next little while," she said. "And accept that not everyone gets a happily-ever-after."

She gave her mom a quick hug and then hurried across the porch into the house.

Agnes stayed on the porch and looked up into the night sky, like black silk with tiny diamonds scattered across it. She took a deep breath, inhaling the rich scents of a late summer night and the dewy moisture of the morning soon to be. Even though she'd had an encounter with the demon just a few hours earlier, this place, her back porch, held no residual fear or apprehension. She was safe here.

She sat down at the top of the steps, rested her elbows on her knees and her chin in her hands. Her sigh was deep, yet soft, and she brushed an errant tear away from her cheek. She'd always wanted, always hoped, that her daughters would have more choices than she. Always prayed that they would find true love, partners who adored them, and respected them. Partners who could be with them forever.

For a moment, she allowed herself to remember her first love. He had been gentle and strong, compassionate and wise, and they had been devoted to each other. But they both understood the ramifications of the curse and the obligations of her heritage. They stayed together as long as they could and finally, as Catalpa grew in her belly, they had to say good-bye.

She returned to her home, this home, her safe place. And Catalpa had been born under this roof.

She remembered when she first held her daughter, the result of their union, she was surprised to feel the instantaneous love for this tiny person blossom in her heart. But she could admit to herself, here in the early hours before dawn, that another part of her heart had never healed. The sorrow from being separated from her first love never quite went away. No matter how much love had grown, there would always be a barren part of her soul, longing for what never could be.

266

She sighed again, but this time, the sadness was for her oldest daughter. She knew how much Cat loved Donovan. She knew that it was the kind of love that wasn't going to go away, no matter how logical Cat tried to make it seem. And she prayed that her daughter would be spared the same sorrow she'd carried all these years.

Chapter Forty-five

"Where's the puppy?" Rowan asked Cat and Hazel as they entered the living room a half-hour later.

"Fuzzy's watching him," Hazel said with a smile. "And he's not too happy about it."

"Who he?" Rowan asked. "Fuzzy or Donovan?"

"Both," Hazel snickered. "But Fuzzy has the upper hand, or should I saw upper paw? Every time Donovan tries to escape, Fuzzy plants a paw on him and holds that little wriggling body in place."

Rowan laughed. "Do you think Donovan is ever going to forgive you," she chuckled, but her laughter stopped when she saw the look of pain in her older sister's eyes. She reached out her hand and placed it gently on Cat's arm. "Cat…I'm sorry."

Cat shrugged and pasted a smile on her face. "No. I'm good, really," she said. "I just want to get through all of this, so our lives can get back to normal."

Hazel shrugged. "Well, as normal as they've ever been," she agreed. "So, what's next?"

"We need to form a circle," Agnes said, coming into the room. "Hazel, could you take care of the rug. Cat, the candles, and Rowan make sure we're safe."

Hazel levitated the large oak table that stood over the huge braided rug and moved it into the corner of the room. Then, with a twist of her hand, the rug rolled itself into a tight roll and slipped against another wall revealing a Celtic knot design that was carved into the old wood floor.

Cat moved four, five-foot-tall, ornately crafted, black cast-iron candlesticks to the outer points of the quaternary knots. The thick wax candles were white and, when Cat lit them, the flames were golden yellow.

While her sisters were occupied, Rowan closed her eyes and envisioned a shimmering bubble encompassing the house, protecting all within and keeping all danger out. Then she toured the house in her mind, looking for anything that might contain darkness or evil.

She breathed easily once she was satisfied that the house was safe, opened her eyes, and smiled at her mother. "We're good," she said.

"Thank you, girls," Agnes said, smiling at each of her daughters individually. "Now, before we begin this session, I need to warn you that I'm not comfortable with what you want to do."

"Mom, we need to find out what the Spiritualists did in the ballroom to learn how to fight against it," Cat reasoned. "I agree there's a risk, but there's a greater risk if we don't know."

Hazel pulled a granola bar from her pocket and took a bite. "Besides," she said. "Not only are we going to be safe in the circle, but Patience is also going with us."

Agnes turned to Rowan. "Did Patience agree to this?" she asked.

Rowan nodded. "Yes, Patience agreed to guide us and introduce us to the spirits in the room," she replied. "She knew these people, and they knew her, so we think we'll get even more information with Patience with us."

Agnes exhaled slowly and then nodded. "Well, I suppose you're right," she said. "I will stay and watch over things here. But if there is a speck of concern or modicum of trouble, you all come back instantly. And you must be back before the dawn, so that gives you about an hour, understood?"

The three sisters nodded.

"Fine," Agnes said, stepping into the knot and taking her place on the eastern-most corner. "We can begin. I will offer the incantation."

Agnes lifted her hand, and a smudge stick appeared in it. She lifted it high above her head, a wisping, gray trail of smoke in the air behind it, and then drew a straight line down. "I cleanse the space to the east."

Catalpa, standing in the next clockwise space, lifted her smudge stick and said, "I cleanse the space to the south."

Hazel, in the next space, also lifted her smudge stick in the same manner. "I cleanse the space to the west," she repeated.

Then Rowan echoed the same actions and said, "I cleanse the space to the north."

When Rowan had finished, all the women turned and walked clockwise around the edge of the knot. With their smudge sticks glowing, they filled the rest of the circle with the gray smoke and chanted, "We cleanse all spaces in between."

Stopping at the places they began, they raised their arms, so the distance between them from fingertip to fingertip was about twelve inches.

"We cast this circle, as is our right," Agnes chanted with her eyes closed. "To protect us with thy holy light. Nothing can harm or corrupt our plea. As we ask, so mote it be."

A beam of ultraviolet light appeared above Agnes and then traveled down from the top of her head and through her arms. The light traveled through her to Rowan and Catalpa on either side of her, through them and then finally to Hazel. The light was warm and bright and lit the inside of the circle with a golden glow.

Agnes opened her eyes and smiled lovingly at her daughters. "Well done," she said softly. "Now we are protected, so we can begin the spell." She looked into the center of the circle. "Patience Goodfellow, we invite your presence."

Instantly, the spirit of Patience, who had been Rowan's spirit guide since she was born, appeared before them. "Well met, my sisters," Patience said. "Are you ready for your journey?"

"Not yet," Hazel said, positioning herself comfortably on a pillow. "I need to make sure my body's comfortable before I leave. Pregnancy's hard enough; I don't need a stiff neck on top of it."

As Hazel shifted into a reclining position, Rowan and Cat sat down in a Lotus position and rested their hands on their knees.

Agnes glanced around the circle, ensuring that her daughters were comfortable and then closed her eyes to recite the incantation.

"Before the dawn, before the light,

273

Their spirits must wander through the night,

To those who summoned the entity,

As I ask, so mote it be."

Suddenly, the spirits of all three girls stood next to Patience in the middle of the circle. They smiled at their mother and then, linking hands with each other and Patience, they vanished from her sight.

Agnes sat still, watching the bodies of her daughters in their restful state, and praying that their spirits would be safe in the spirit realm.

Chapter Forty-six

Cat hadn't traveled through the spirit realm in a long time. She glanced around at all the shadowy figures that occupied the dimension that was on the other side of the veil from life. Movement was quick and purposeful, as spirits moved past her in a blur, eager to get to their next destination. She noticed a bright glow out of the corner of her eye and turned to gaze at it, as she was pulled along by Patience and her sisters.

"Heaven," she whispered, staring at the light.

It would be so easy to let go of Hazel's hand and just float toward the light. It would be peaceful there; she just knew it. She would be surrounded by love, and she wouldn't have to worry anymore.

Suddenly, their forward movement stopped, and when Cat looked around, Patience was standing in front of her. Her eyes were filled with sympathy and sadness. She didn't speak, but Cat could hear Patience's voice in her head.

"I've been dead for a long time," she whispered. "And one of the most important things I've learned from the spirits I interact with is that anyone who chose to come before their time carries with them a mountain of regret."

Cat shook her head, glancing beyond Patience to the bright light in the distance.

"But it's so beautiful and peaceful there," Cat argued.

Patience nodded. "Yes, it is," she agreed. "When you're taken at the right time. But when you go early, you're responsible for the grief and pain your family and friends feel. You're responsible for the problems that have gone unresolved. You're responsible for the things you were supposed to accomplish."

Cat sighed and nodded. "I didn't realize," she said sadly.

"And," Patience added with gentle sympathy. "What's usually the worst part, is that you realize the pain you'd been going through was only temporary and there were wonderful things in store for you in your future, and you denied yourself that joy."

"It doesn't seem temporary," Cat admitted.

Patience laughed softly. "That's because you're still on human time," she replied. "Eternal time gives you a whole different perspective about things. Now, are you ready to continue? Because I can promise you, this problem cannot be solved without your help."

Cat glanced over at her sisters, who were waiting patiently in front of them. "How could I have even considered hiding away in heaven when I know what's at stake for my family?" she asked Patience.

"When we're overwhelmed, we're often tempted by what seems to be an easier solution," Patience explained. "Usually, that's the time when we need to stop and allow ourselves a moment to reflect and rest. And remember what's important to us."

Cat nodded. "I'm ready," she said firmly. "Thank you for your help."

"It was my pleasure," Patience replied. "And now, we need to hurry."

They continued, but this time, Cat didn't allow her vision to stray and kept her eyes firmly focused in the direction Patience was leading them. Suddenly, they were no longer in the hazy portals of the spirit realm, they were inside the B&B on the third-floor level, and there were a group of other spirits dressed in old-fashioned clothing standing together in the center of the room.

"I don't feel good about this," a portly older gentleman was stating. "We need to leave it to the Willoughbys to fix this. We've done enough damage."

The bitter laughter of one of the women drew Cat's immediate attention. She looked familiar. Where had she seen her before?

"The Willoughbys are not the saviors everyone thinks they are," the woman snapped. "Many of us feel this entity would offer us help to protect many of the downtrodden and misunderstood in our community. The Willoughby's are imposing their will on the rest of us."

278

Hazel turned and looked at Cat, her eyes wide. "Wanda," she mouthed.

Cat immediately pictured the peroxide-blonde floosy who was part of the other coven in Whitewater.

"Now, Mistress Wildes," the old man continued, confirming that this was indeed Wanda's ancestor. "The Willoughbys are risking their lives for us. For all of us."

Mistress Wildes smiled, and Cat immediately recognized the manipulative maneuver. "Well, of course they are," the woman cooed. "And I just think we need to do all we can to help them. This spell I've put together will bind the entity and help them send it away. Perhaps by doing this, we can save the Willoughby sisters lives."

"And you think it will help them?" the man asked. "It might save them?"

"Why else would I even consider doing it?" Mistress Wildes replied innocently. "I've not only created an incantation to bind the entity, but I've also created an amulet to increase the power we have over the entity."

The old man sighed and nodded his head. "Very well," he said sadly. "Very well, we will work together to bind the entity in order to save the Willoughbys."

Mistress Wildes smiled widely. "You won't regret this, Dr. Pratt. You won't regret this at all. Now everyone, quickly, enter into a circle and hold hands while I read the spell."

Chapter Forty-seven

Finias, Henry, and Joseph sat around a large library table, each with a stack of books next to them, scanning pages of diaries and composition books. Joseph finished another one, closed the marbled black and white cover and moved it into the already-read pile. He ran his hands through his hair and sat back in his chair.

"This is ridiculous," he stated, bringing the heads of the other two men up and out of the books they were reading.

"What?" Henry asked.

"Trying to find any useful information from these stacks of useless prattle," Joseph replied.

Henry judiciously placed a sheet of paper between the pages of the journal he'd been reading and also sat up, stretching his back and his neck along the way. "I don't know," he said with a wry smile. "I've encountered several recipes for herbal ointments I'm going to share with Rowan, a spell for curing a dry cow, and some juicy

281

gossip about the women who run the millinery. Who knew that hats could be so scandalous?"

"And that's just what I mean," Joseph said. "We might be wasting our time here. There might not be any information about what happened in the upper rooms of the academy in this entire library. We should be doing more."

"Often, it's the little things that bring us the greater rewards," Finias said.

Joseph rolled his eyes and sent Finias a look of exasperation. "Okay, that's something that I could find inside a Fortune cookie. It's not what I want to hear when we are trying to save the lives of the Willoughbys."

The rattle of the doorknob silenced them all immediately, and Joseph carefully lowered his hand to the gun in his holster. All eyes were locked on the door as it slowly opened, and a petite, older woman stepped inside. She looked around at the men, and calmly shook her head.

"Well, I certainly didn't expect to find you in my library," she scolded. "The proper action would have been to ask permission."

"Mrs. Anderson?" Henry asked, recognizing the woman as the one who'd guarded his family's grimoire. "Charity Pratt Anderson? Do you remember me?"

She looked at Henry and smiled. "Why, of course," she said eagerly. "You are a Goodfellow, are you not?"

He nodded. "My mother was a Goodfellow," he agreed. "I'm Henry Goodfellow McDermott."

"And why are you in my library in the middle of the night?" she asked him.

"We are still working on finding a solution to ending the curse," Henry explained. "And we believe that something happened in the special room of the Pratt Institute. Something that might have bound the demon to that house."

Her eyes widened, and she nodded slowly. "So, it is true," she exclaimed softly. "I'd read rumors, but I

283

never thought…I mean, I'd hoped that my ancestor had not allowed such dark magic to happen within the walls of the academy."

"What happened?" Finias asked.

Charity turned to him and straightened herself up to her full five-foot height. "I don't believe we've been introduced," she replied coolly.

"Forgive me," Henry inserted. "Charity Pratt Anderson, this is Ellis Thomas, a colleague of mine, and this is Police Chief Joseph Norwalk. We have been working together to find a solution for the Willoughbys."

Her reserve diminished, and she smiled cordially at the other two men. "Well, truly, if you had just called me, I could have saved you quite a bit of time," she said, hurrying to the furthest set of shelves and pulling out a large leather-bound book that resembled a family Bible. "When I found these journals, I knew they had to be placed in a special place. If not only for the preservation of the Pratt's good name."

She carried the book to the table and lifted the front cover. The inside of the book was hollow, and a dusty, leather bound journal lay at the bottom of the cavity. Charity reached inside and gently took out the book. "This was my great-great-great grandfather's journal," she explained. "Morris Pratt. And he wrote about the binding spell in this journal."

"So, there was a binding spell," Finias said softly. "That answers a lot of questions."

Charity held the book to her chest. "Well, perhaps not," she said sadly. "Morris discovered that he'd been fooled. Mistress Wildes didn't bind the demon; she gave him more power."

"Wildes?" Joseph exclaimed. "As in the Wildes Coven?"

Charity nodded. "Yes, Mistress Wildes was one of the witches who felt they could use the power of the demon to curtail the persecution of their kind," she said. "And, after having researched this for years, I've come to believe she and others like her, wanted to use some of that power to exact revenge."

"May I see the entry?" Henry asked.

With just a moment's hesitation, Charity handed the book to Henry and sighed with reassurance when he pulled out his handkerchief and covered his hands, so the oils from his fingers didn't mar the leather covering of the old journal. He delicately opened the cover and looked down at the yellowing pages. "What's the date of the entry?" he asked.

"October 28th," Charity replied. "Three days before Samhain."

"Ah, three days," Finias added. "How ironic."

"What's ironic about three days?" Joseph asked.

"In scripture, the number three signifies completeness or perfection," Finias replied. "Throughout the Old and New Testament, three days signified an important event."

"So, they were mocking the Bible?" Joseph asked.

Finias shrugged. "Or they were trying to pull on power that was not theirs to use," he said. "Three days also points to most acts of divine intervention that impacts the history of mankind."

Henry carefully turned to the entry dated October 28th. "I have it," he said, looking down at the faded handwriting. "Let me try and read it to you."

"I am ashamed to confess that I have allowed myself and the Academy to be used for evil purposes. Mistress Wildes, claiming that she wanted to help the Willoughbys in their quest to imprison the demon, instead created a spell and an amulet that would, instead, offer the demon greater power and an eventual release from its confinement."

Henry looked up at Joseph and Finias. "This could be why the demon was able to use its power and influence people before Samhain."

He looked down and continued reading.

"We created the circle and cleared the space with sage, as we have done in the past. Mistress Wildes moved

from the edge of the circle to the middle and took several

things from the pockets of her robe. She placed a small

earthen bowl in the middle of the floor, then she laid a

thin lead tablet with etching on it inside the bowl.

Afterwards she sprinkled some concoction made from

herbs and other things on top of the tablet. To the best of

my memory, this is the incantation she chanted:

> *We summon the sacred power of three,*
>
> *To diminish the spell they create for thee,*
>
> *The sisters will try, but will not succeed,*
>
> *As I demand, so mote it be.*

As soon as we understood what she was saying, it

took us a moment to reconcile ourselves to her betrayal,

and then we all jumped forward to stop her. But it was too

late. The lead tablet, with what I now understand was the

spell etched onto it, had melted in the bowl along with

special herbs for protection and remnants of pieces of hair

and clothing from the Willoughby sisters.

We were able to restrain Mistress Wildes and

keep her secured until after Samhain, but I believe the

damage had already been done. The Willoughbys now had

a more powerful enemy on their hands. I confiscated the

amulet and hid it away. I know it holds great power, and I

will not risk that it will be used for evil."

Chapter Forty-eight

Cat, Hazel, Patience, and Rowan watched as the scene Henry had just read at the library of the museum was played out before them.

"Big surprise, a Wildes lied," Hazel said.

"Not a surprise," Cat said. "But a game changer. Did the sisters know about the spell?"

Patience shook her head. "As far as I know, there was no mention of another spell," she said, her eyes wide with concern. "This could change everything."

"What do you mean?" Rowan asked.

"The spells in the grimoire that were used to guide you were based on only one spell imprisoning the demon," Patience explained. "Because of this extra spell, lessening the sisters' powers, everything we thought we could do has changed."

Cat turned quickly, watching the ghost of Morris Pratt hurry to the middle of the circle and pick something up. "What's that?" she asked, as he hurried toward the fireplace.

"We have to go," Patience interrupted. "It's nearly dawn."

"But, wait, Professor Pratt has something in his hands," Cat argued.

Suddenly, the spirit of Mistress Wildes turned and looked directly at Patience and the sisters. "I know who you are, and I know what you are trying to do," she said to them. "But you will not triumph this time. The sisters died in vain, and so will you."

Anger overwhelmed Cat at Mistress Wildes mocking smile. "You're not going to win," Cat said. "We know about your betrayal."

Mistress Wildes laughed. "And you will take that knowledge with you to the grave."

"Cat now!" Patience exclaimed, grabbing hold of Cat's hand. "We need to go now!"

Suddenly, Cat found herself being pulled away from the room and back into the spirit realm along with her sisters.

"Patience," Cat began to complain, turning toward Rowan's spirit guide.

"Hurry!" Patience shouted, and Cat was surprised at the vehemence in her voice. Patience was always calm.

"What…" Cat began.

"He's here," Patience said, her voice shaking. "We have to run!"

Cat glanced over her shoulder and saw a swirling, dark substance snake around the area they'd just come from. It wove around, like a black cloud in the shape of a serpent, entering and exiting the room they'd been in.

She turned back and pushed forward, with little success. Running in the spirit realm was like running in waist deep water; her forward motion was slowed by the atmosphere around her. "This isn't working," Cat cried out, her thoughts touching her sisters' minds.

"We've got to keep going," Rowan replied. "We don't have any choice."

Cat glanced over her shoulder again and wished she hadn't. The serpent had turned away from the outside of the room and was now slithering in their direction.

"He sees us," Cat warned. "And he's headed in our direction."

"He can't hurt us," Hazel said. "Right, Patience?"

"We're in his realm right now," Patience replied. "We need to hurry!"

"Crap!" Hazel responded. "He's gaining on us, and we're running through oatmeal. Isn't there anything we can do?"

"Our magic isn't going to work here," Rowan said.

"We're almost back," Patience said, releasing Cat's hand. "Just keep going straight ahead, to that portal."

"Wait, where are you going?" Cat asked.

Patience smiled at her. "I'm already dead," she said, moving behind her. "He can't hurt me. Now run!"

The sisters ran forward, and Cat glanced behind once more to see Patience step in front of the swirling dark mass. She held up her hands and light shone from them. The darkness was deterred for only a moment but then surged forward, wrapping itself around the gentle guide.

Cat saw brief bursts of light escaping from the dark swirling mass; then there was only darkness. The serpent uncoiled itself and pushed forward, towards them.

"Just a few more steps," Rowan cried.

"Hurry!" Cat screamed from the back, as the darkness was nearly upon them.

"Jump!" Hazel cried.

They woke up, their hearts pounding, and they gasped for breath as their spirits reunited with their bodies.

"What happened?" Agnes asked. "Are you alright?"

Cat shook her head as she tried to speak but failed. Suddenly, the puppy dashed into the room with Fuzzy chasing close behind. The puppy ran to Cat's side and stood up, its paws on her shoulders, licking her cheek. "I'm okay," she finally panted. "I'm okay."

Then the puppy sat down and began to bark angrily at her.

Cat rolled her eyes and waved her arms in exasperation, immediately Donovan, the man, was sitting on the floor in front of her. "And another thing," he shouted. "What the hell were you thinking going off like that without one of us..."

He looked around and then looked down at himself. "I'm not a dog!" he exclaimed. "Why not?"

"Because we're going to need everyone we can get to fight this thing," Cat said, as she stood up and moved away from him. Then she turned back and met his eyes. "And that still might not be enough."

Chapter Forty-nine

"We need to find that amulet," Henry said, as he took a picture of the page, carefully closed the journal, and handed it back to Charity. "It could be the key."

"I'm afraid I've searched for that amulet for years," Charity interrupted. "I've gone through all of Morris' belongings and all through the records and boxes that came from the Academy when it was closed down. I have never been able to find it."

"Perhaps it wasn't ready to be found yet," he countered. "Would you mind…"

He stopped when his phone rang, and he looked down at the screen. "It's Agnes," he said before he answered the phone.

"Agnes," he began. "What? How? Are they okay?"

Joseph and Finias were already on their feet coming towards him. Henry hung up the phone and turned to Charity. "I'm afraid we have to leave," he said to her. "There's been a complication with the Willoughbys."

"Oh, I'm so sorry," Charity replied.

"Thank you," Henry replied, standing up and hurrying past her. "We will be in touch."

Once out of the library, they ran across the main room of the museum and out the door.

"What?" Joseph called as they ran to his cruiser.

"They took a trip through the spirit realm," Henry said, increasing his pace. "It didn't end well."

Joseph unlocked the car and the men dove inside, still fastening their seat belts when Joseph accelerated down the road, his lights flashing. "What the hell do you mean, it didn't end well?" Joseph asked. "Hazel?"

"All of the sisters are fine," Henry began, then he shook his head. "Actually, that's not right. They are devastated but physically unharmed. However, they lost Patience."

"Who is Patience?" Finias asked.

Henry took a deep breath. "Patience is Rowan's spirit guide, and she is also my great-great-grandmother."

"I don't understand. How did they lose her?" Joseph asked.

"Agnes didn't give me much more information than that," Henry said. "She just told me to hurry."

Joseph increased the acceleration and turned on the sirens as they drove out of the city towards the Willoughby farm. "Why would they take risks like that?" he muttered. "Why the hell didn't they wait."

"Because they understand that this is their fight, their obligation," Finias said.

"Well, they're going to have to change their way of thinking," Joseph growled, smacking the steering wheel with his fist. "They're going to damn well change their way of thinking. We are in this together. We are all in this together."

"Even more so than before," Finias added.

Henry turned to Finias. "What do you mean?" he asked.

"If the original sisters didn't know about the spell, whatever incantation they cast of the demon is flawed," Finias replied. "Whatever plan they'd conjured for the past hundred years is incorrect. Whatever assurances they had of defeating this creature have been cancelled. This is a whole new game now."

"So, no more three from one?" Joseph asked.

Finias shook his head. "No, the three from one could have worked had the original incantation been binding. But now, because of the Wildes Witch, this is all out warfare."

"Which is why the demon had been trying to recruit members of the opposing coven," Henry said. "He realizes that this is a war – a new war – not just the climax of an old spell."

Finias nodded. "And this is why we need a whole new game plan, comprised of many more than just the three."

"The grimoire had already told us that the three would each need another one," Henry said. "A partner in this fight."

Finias nodded. "But did the grimoire tell you that the fight might begin before Samhain?"

"What?" Joseph asked. "What are you talking about?"

"Look at the moon," Finias replied.

They looked out the cruiser's window and saw the low hanging full moon encircled by a blood red haze.

"What does that mean?" Henry asked. "That wasn't like that earlier."

"Things have changed. The demon is summoning his followers for a battle," Finias said. "A blood red haze around the moon means an impending attack. They plan to strike tonight."

"What the hell are we supposed to do?" Joseph asked, turning onto the road that led to the Willoughby farm.

"We need the amulet," Finias said. "If we can destroy it, we can reduce the demon's power." He looked at Henry. "Is there a vehicle I can borrow once we get to the Willoughby's farm?"

Henry nodded. "Yes, my car," he said, reaching in his jacket pocket and pulling out the keys. He handed them to Finias. "It's parked next to the barn."

"I'll go back to the B&B and see if I can find anything there," Finias said. "And you find out everything you can from the sisters and their experience. Call me with anything. The smallest detail might be our saving grace."

Joseph turned the cruiser into the driveway of the Willoughby farm and pulled behind the house. Immediately, Finias jumped out of the cruiser and ran across the barnyard to Henry's car. He slipped into the driver's seat, started the car, and pulled away in a matter of moments.

Henry and Joseph dashed up the back stairs without giving Finias another thought. Their focus was on getting inside.

Henry pushed the door open and hurried into the living room. In the corner of the room in an overstuffed chair, Rowan was huddled in a fetal position, sobbing softly. He paused for only a moment, then moved to her side. Placing his hand on her arm, he gently whispered her name.

She turned to him, her eyes filled with tears, her face filled with sorrow. "Oh, Henry," she sobbed. "She's gone. Patience is gone. And she's gone because of us."

He wrapped his arms around her and just held her. "I'm so sorry," he whispered, pressing a kiss against her head. She burrowed against his shoulder, her tears soaking his shirt.

"She was protecting us," she cried, "from the demon."

Henry's heart clenched for a moment, suddenly realizing the danger they had all been in. "What happened?" he asked when he could trust his voice.

Rowan took a deep, shuddering breath and looked up at him. His face filled with concern, he withdrew his handkerchief and gently blotted her face. "Tell me," he pleaded.

"We watched the incantation," Rowan said, her voice still shaking.

"With Mistress Wildes?" Henry asked.

Rowan's tear-filled eyes widened. "How did you know?"

"We found Morris Pratt's journal at the museum," he replied. "He wrote about the incantation and the amulet."

Rowan nodded slowly. "As soon as we learned what had happened, Patience was adamant that we leave immediately," she said. "She realized that we were in danger because of the spell that Mistress Wildes had cast.

Cat wanted to try and find the amulet, but Patience insisted we leave."

Taking a deep, shuddering breath, Rowan continued. "We saw him, in the guise of a black serpent, as soon as we left the B&B. Once Patience saw him, she told us to run. But he was getting closer."

She shook her head, and tears flowed freely once again. "She told us to go ahead, and then she confronted him," she wept softly. "He just swirled around her, like a snake with its prey, and then she disappeared in a burst of light."

"So, she distracted him and then went to the light?" he asked.

"What?" Rowan asked, confused.

"Well, since she was already a spirit of light, he had no control over her," Henry said. "Right?"

"I suppose," Rowan replied thoughtfully.

"So, she distracted him for enough time for you to arrive back safely, and then she moved to the light," he surmised. "At least that's how I think it works."

304

She smiled at him. "So, she's not gone?" she asked.

He shrugged. "Well, I don't know all the rules from that side," he confessed. "She might have given up her ability to be your spirit guide, but she's certainly not in a bad place. The demon lost control over her once she died."

She leaned over and placed a gentle kiss on his lips. "Thank you," she said, taking a deep breath. "I feel much better now."

He leaned over and kissed her back. "Better?" he asked softly.

She took another breath and nodded. "A little. I'm going to miss her. She has always been a huge part of my life," she answered truthfully. "But I know crying isn't going to help us right now."

He hugged her to him and placed a kiss on her forehead. "No, but remembering her and honoring her sacrifice will help," he said. "Ready to go forward in battle, for Patience?"

She smiled back. "For Patience!" she replied with firm resolve. "Yes! For Patience!"

Chapter Fifty

Hazel walked into the kitchen and saw Donovan sitting at the counter, eating a sandwich.

"What? No kibble?" she asked, slipping into the stool next to him and taking one of his potato chips.

He grimaced at her and shook his head. "I'm still finding fleas," he complained with a grin. "So, hungry?" He offered her the other half of his sandwich.

"Always," she replied, accepting it and taking a big bite. "This pregnancy stuff is brutal."

He shook his head. "I still can't believe you're pregnant," he said. "You're too little."

"Obviously not," she said as she chewed. "So, you are still in the doghouse?"

"Are we going to continue with these canine jokes for a while?" he replied.

She grinned and nodded. "Until we are both sick of them."

He raised his hand. "I'm sick of them," he said.

She shrugged. "Well, lucky for both of us, I'm still highly amused," she said. "So, what's up?"

"I don't know," he replied. "Cat won't talk to me about it. How can I help if I don't know what to do?"

"It's all about the amulet," Hazel said, taking another bite of the sandwich. "I guess we're all pretty freaked out about it."

"What amulet?" Donovan asked.

"The amulet that Mistress Wildes made for the demon at the Academy before the sisters enchanted him and imprisoned him for one hundred years," she explained. "The amulet gives him more power."

Donovan's jaw dropped, and he nodded slowly. "I've heard about it," he said, he concentrated for a moment. "As a matter of fact, when he was inside of me, I saw it. It's hidden in the ballroom."

Hazel's eyes widened, and she put the sandwich down. "You saw it?" she asked. "You know where it is?"

308

He nodded slowly. "Yeah, I think I do," he said. "But it's a picture memory; I'm going to have to go there and find it myself."

He stood up, and Hazel jumped off her stool and put her hand on his shoulder. "Wait, what are you doing?" she asked.

He looked down at her. "Remember that trick I taught you years ago?" he asked.

"Transporting yourself places?" she asked with a smile. "Yeah, I use it all the time."

"I'm going to the ballroom to look around," he said.

"Wait! You need backup," she said.

He shook his head. "It will take too long for anyone else to get there," he replied. "I'm good."

She shook her head. "No way," she said. "You could still be under his influence, and you could end up giving him the amulet. Then where would we be? I'm going with you."

"No, you're pregnant," he argued.

309

"Yeah, and if we don't get the amulet in a couple of weeks, I could be dead," she replied. "See, easy choice. Besides, I can grab it from you and bring it back home in case we're interrupted."

He sighed and shook his head. "I'm going to regret this, I know it," he said.

"The only regret you'll have is that you didn't think of it first," she replied. "Now come on, we've got a treasure to find."

She grabbed the sandwich and took one more bite, then set it down. "Ready," she said, through a mouthful of food and grabbed his hands.

"Okay," he replied. "Let's go."

A moment later, the kitchen was deserted except for two plates with half-eaten sandwiches on them.

Chapter Fifty-one

"Okay, this place looks just as creepy in real life as it did when we were in the spirit realm," Hazel said as they reappeared in the ballroom.

She looked around at the exposed pipes, the cracking paint, and the peeling woodwork, then turned to Donovan. "You know, I could have this whole place remodeled and looking like something straight out of HGTV just like that," she said, snapping her fingers in the air.

Donovan shook his head. "Concentrate Hazel," he said. "We need to find that amulet."

She shook her head. "No, you need to find that amulet," she said. "I'm here for back-up, good looks, and a speedy getaway. But, in the meantime, I can dream, can't I?"

"As long as you do it quietly while I concentrate," he replied, a smile softening his words.

"I can be quiet," she replied with a smirk. "When I want to."

She strolled across the room to examine the tall windows while Donovan walked over to the white-brick fireplace on the opposite wall. He closed his eyes and tried to picture where he'd seen the amulet. He placed his hand on the fireplace front and held it there, trying to sense any residual magic. He moved his hand to the right, paused, and then returned it to his starting point. Yes! There was definitely a change in vibrations.

He moved it further to the left and could now feel the thrumming, like a heartbeat, in his hand. Low, but steady. He continued to move his hand along the brick work, first to the left and then down, towards the hearth. Even though his own heart was beating with excitement, his movements were careful and steady as he made his way towards what he was sure was the hidden compartment housing the amulet.

Hazel walked slowly from one corner of the room to the other. She checked the plaster walls for structural integrity, checked the floors for warping, and was starting to check the windowsills for dry rot when she noticed a darkening on one of the walls.

Curious, she began to move towards it, then stopped as she realized the dark spot was growing. In a matter of moments, the three-inch diameter spot was now 12-inches and expanding.

"This can not be good," she said, her voice hoarse and frightened. She backed away from the spot toward Donovan.

"Donovan," she tried to cry out, but her throat was too dry to make much noise. "Donovan."

"Busy here," Donovan replied easily, as he moved his hand closer to the prize.

"Donovan," she squeaked, backing into him.

He turned in exasperation. "What? I'm nearly there," he said, then he saw the look on her face and spun around. "Oh, crap!"

The dark spot was now 24 inches in diameter, and the wall was bulging out. "I think it's…" Hazel gulped.

313

"Yeah, it's him," Donovan said. "And he's probably not happy with what we're doing."

"I thought he was, like, smoke," she said, still staring at the bulging wall.

"I think he decided to make it real," Donovan replied. "Tangible can cause a lot more damage than black smoke, and the only way he can pick up the amulet is to be real."

"The bulge is getting bigger," Hazel warned him. "You'd better hurry."

He turned back and stuck his hand underneath the front of the brick, into the flue and felt around. His fingers caught on a small indentation in the rock. He pressed on it and heard the click of a lock. Suddenly, a piece of brick sprung forward, and something fell into his hands.

"Got it," he whispered, looking at the soot covered object. He turned around and pressed it into Hazel's hands. "You've got to go sweetheart."

She shook her head as the serpent pushed through the plaster and hissed at them. "I can't leave you here," she argued.

"Donovan," the serpent hissed, as it unwound itself to its full height of ten feet. "Bring it to me."

"You can't fight this thing by yourself," Hazel whispered.

"The important thing here is the amulet," he whispered to her. "I'll come after you soon, but I need to stall him and give you a head start."

Donovan turned to the serpent. "Bring what to you?" he asked, holding out his hands. "I've got nothing."

"I control you, Donovan," the creature hissed. "I am part of you. You can feel the excitement of my darkness. And this amulet will bring us more excitement, more darkness, and more power."

Donovan could feel the tug in the pit of his stomach, and his palms began to sweat. "Go!" he whispered harshly. "Go now!"

"You won't let him win!" Hazel insisted. "You won't let him control you!"

He took a deep breath, seeing not only the pleading, but also the concern in her eyes, and the tug inside his gut lessoned. "I won't," he said, taking a sigh of relief. "I won't."

"Donovan!" the creature screamed as it realized its effect on Donovan was fading. "Take it from her!"

Her eyes wide with fear, she stared at him. "Promise?"

He nodded. "Promise," he replied, hoping he would be able to keep his word. "Now go!"

She screamed as the serpent flew towards them and disappeared before her scream had finished echoing in the room.

Chapter Fifty-two

The sun was just peaking above the tops of the buildings in downtown Whitewater when Finias made it back to the B&B. He parked Henry's car in the parking lot and quietly let himself in through the front door and stole up the stairs to the second floor. He paused, looking longingly at his bedroom and the hot shower that awaited him after this long night, then shook his head.

"No, first things first," he said softly.

Walking to the door to the third floor, he easily unlocked it and softly ascended the stairs. The chains strung through the handles that closed off the ballroom only took a moment to unwind, and Finias carefully laid them on the old carpeting in the hallway. He had just grasped the door handle firmly when he heard the scream. Yanking it open, he watched in shock as the serpent lunged towards Donovan.

"Bacainn!" Donovan cried out, and the serpent smashed against an invisible wall.

Finias ran to Donovan's side. "Was that for show or are you really on our side?" he asked.

Donovan looked at him in astonishment. "Are you kidding me?" he yelled as the serpent pulled back and hissed at him, venom dripping off his fangs.

"I will kill you, traitor!" the serpent hissed.

Finias looked at the demon and nodded. "Okay, I believe you," he said. "Now what?"

The serpent attacked again and this time, nearly broke through the wall Donovan had put up. "He's strong," Donovan said. "And this wall isn't going to last forever."

"How long do we have to fight him?" Finias asked.

Donovan met his eyes and lowered his voice. "Until the Willoughbys have a chance to destroy the amulet," he said meaningfully.

"You found it?" Finias asked, astonished.

"Just moments before he appeared," Donovan replied, watching the creature pull back for another attack.

"Hazel took it home, so we just have to keep him busy for a while."

"You will not be able to destroy it," the creature taunted. "The magic is too strong!"

Finias smiled and nodded. Then he called out, "Gladius mortis."

Immediately two machete-like swords appeared in his hands. He handed one to Donovan and nodded. "This is how we kill snakes in the forests of my homeland," he said.

Donovan hefted the sword in his hand, testing its weight, and then sliced it through the air several times. "Nice," he agreed. "Let's see how it works on house snakes."

The serpent lunged again, and this time, the barrier failed. Donovan grabbed the hilt with both hands and brought the sword around, swinging into the side of the creature's face. Hissing in pain, the serpent tried to retreat, but Finias stepped up and struck it near the base of its skull. Its body whirled and its massive tail swept across the floor, knocking both men off their feet.

Donovan sat up quickly and shook his head. "Forgot about the tail," he said, jumping to his feet in time to block the serpent's fangs with the sword. A clang echoed in the room as the steel from the sword hit the ivory of the fang.

Finias got up, a little slower than Donovan, and shook his head. "I did much better in my younger days," he admitted. He brought the sword up over his shoulder and then brought it down swiftly on the serpent's tail. Green ooze spilled out from the wound, flooding the floor.

Donovan jumped back and turned to Finias. "Was that planned, or did you think we needed a greater challenge?"

Finias chuckled softly and nodded. "Well, it was two against one."

The serpent reared back and lunged again. Donovan countered, bringing his sword down across its nose. It retreated to the corner of the room, swirling and hissing, as green ooze seeped from several wounds.

"We need to keep him busy here with us," Donovan said.

"No problem," Finias replied, moving forward, his sword poised for attack.

Donovan mirrored Finias' stance, and they both approached the serpent, intent on doing more damage. Suddenly, the serpent turned away and dove through the opening in the wall. "We attack this day, Donovan! You and the Willoughby witches will die," the serpent screamed.

"No!" Finias cried, running forward, trying to catch hold of the creature.

"Claude ostium," Donovan cried, ordering the portal to close.

The opening immediately closed up, leaving the last two feet of the serpent writhing on the floor. Finias stabbed it through, and the tail finally stopped moving.

"Well, the tail's dead," Donovan said, wiping the sweat from his brow. "But the rest of the creature is alive and well. I wonder what he's planning to do now."

"The moon this morning had a red haze around it," Finias explained. "Foreshadowing a battle this evening."

Donovan ran to the window and shook his head. "This is Whitewater," he said with dread. "We don't wait until dark for anything."

Suddenly, the sky darkened, and a black cloud in the shape of a serpent circled the sky. It swirled over the top of the town, its length increasing until it blocked the sun. The wind picked up and whistled through the streets, rattling windows and doors, bending treetops, and churning up dust. Darkness, like the night, enveloped the town.

A sound, carried on the wind, whistled through the room. Donovan felt a chill race down his back. "Do you hear that?" Donovan asked Finias.

"What?" Finias asked, walking over to the window.

They both stood in silence for a moment and then heard the dark whispering that was carried on the wind.

"What is he saying?" Donovan asked.

"The language is old and forbidden," Finias said. "It is a language of ancient spells and secret combinations. He is calling his followers to come to his side. He wants them to retrieve the amulet. But I don't understand why it's so important to him."

Donovan put his hands on his head, searching his memory for anything that could help. Finally, he remembered and turned to Finias, a look of alarm on his face. "The amulet is what gave him the power to influence the minds of the members of the coven," Donovan explained. "And once they followed him, he gained more power. Without its influence, his power will recede until Samhain."

"And he's not the kind of creature to give up power very easily," Finias said. "Where do you think they are going?"

"My best guess would be the Willoughbys," Donovan replied, watching large groups of black-cloaked people coming towards them in every direction. "Here's your red haze around the moon battle."

"Can we get through them?" Finias asked.

Although Donovan knew that he could get to the Willoughbys in moments by transporting, he realized that he would be leaving Finias to fend for himself. And, they could use every able body they could get.

"I know some back roads," Donovan said, deciding to stay with Finias. "We can probably beat this crowd. But…"

"But what?" Finias asked suspiciously.

"Most of those people down there, members of the other covens, still believe that I'm working with the demon," Donovan explained. "In order to get out of town, you're going to need to pretend you're my prisoner."

"I don't feel good about that," Finias said.

Donovan cocked his head toward the window and the crowd filling up the streets. "You got a better idea?" he asked. "One that won't slow us down?"

Finias sighed. "Fine," he said. "But use ropes instead of handcuffs, so I can break free and help if needed."

Donovan nodded. "Deal."

Chapter Fifty-three

Hazel appeared in the kitchen, still shaking from the encounter.

"Where the hell have you been?" Joseph yelled. "Do you know how worried..."

Hazel's tears brought him to a complete stop. "Hazel, sweetheart," he exclaimed, hurrying forward to catch her in his arms. "What's wrong? Are you hurt?"

"I have it," she stammered, holding her hand out. "I have the amulet."

"You have the amulet?" Cat exclaimed, coming into the room with Rowan, Henry, Agnes. "How could you think about doing this by yourself?"

Hazel wiped her tears and took a shaky breath. "I didn't do it by myself," she said, defending herself. "Donovan and I did it. We transported."

Cat was stunned. "Donovan can't transport," she countered.

"Who do you think taught me?" Hazel replied. "But I wasn't supposed to tell anyone. It was our secret."

Cat immediately thought of all those times when she'd dreamt he'd been there, comforting her. Could he have actually come to her? Had he watched over her?

She pushed those thoughts to the side. What was important now was their safety. Donovan's safety. "Where is he now?"

Hazel shook her head. "The serpent...the demon...came through the wall," she said. "Donovan gave me the amulet and told me to take it here, to destroy it. He said he was just going to distract it while I made it home safely. But he should be here by now."

Henry stepped forward and held out his hand. "May I see it?" he asked.

Hazel immediately put the amulet in his hand. "What should we do?"

"We need to reverse the spell and then destroy the amulet," he said. "And the sooner we destroy it, the better chance we all have of winning this fight."

"Can we destroy it without the witch who cast it?" Rowan asked.

"I have the spell," Henry said, then he paused and sighed. "Or at least, I have Morris Pratt's version of the spell."

"We were there," Rowan exclaimed. "We heard her offer it, so between what you have and our memories; we should be able to destroy it."

"Should we destroy it?" Joseph asked.

"What do you mean?" Cat replied. "Of course, we should."

"Not necessarily," Joseph countered. "Amulets are powerful magic. Especially amulets that have been around for this long. Why destroy it? Why not alter it for our good?"

"Alter it?" Agnes asked, nodding her head slowly. "That's an intriguing idea."

Henry turned toward Agnes. "I don't understand," he said.

"Magic isn't inherently good or evil," she explained. "It's just a force. What makes it good or evil is the intent of those who are using it." She looked around the kitchen quickly, trying to find something to illustrate what she was saying, and her eyes fell upon a cast iron frying pan, hanging next to the stove. "Take my cast iron pan. It can be used to make wonderful food or, if wielded like a weapon, it can create quite a dent in someone's head. The pan isn't inherently good or bad; it's what the user does with it. Does that make sense?"

Henry nodded slowly. "And because this magic is so old and was conjured with power, we'll be able to transfer that power into something we can use to fight against the demon?"

"If we do it right," Agnes hedged.

"Ah, there's always a catch," Henry nodded. "And how do we do it right?"

"We study the spell, all of it's elements, and recreate them," Agnes said, "but substitute good intent for evil."

329

"We should also melt it down and reshape it, so the physical is changed as well," Rowan added. "New purpose, new intent, new look."

"What do we need to start?" Henry asked.

"First, I need to know if we have any natural connections to the amulet," Agnes said. "That would make the transfer easier." She turned to Hazel. "How did you find the amulet?"

"Donovan said that he saw it, in his mind," she replied. "He didn't know if it was his memory or something residual from the demon. But he thought he could find it. Then, when we got to the room, he went to the fireplace, and it was like he could feel it. He kept moving his hand on the bricks, closer and closer, until he knew where it was. He reached into the flue, just before the serpent came out of the wall and then he had it in his hand."

"So, Donovan has a link," Cat said. "What does that mean?"

"It would be better for the transfer if he were part of the circle," Agnes said.

"He should have been back already," Hazel said, her voice thick with worry. "He promised me that he would come as soon as I was safe."

Just then, Cat's phone rang. She looked down, and relief swept over her. "It's Donovan," she said, accessing the call. "Hello?"

She listened for a moment, her eyes wide with concern, and then nodded. "Okay, we'll be ready," she said.

She hung up the phone and looked up at her family and friends. "There's an army of members of the coven heading our way," she said. "There was a haze of red around the moon early this morning. The demon is attacking."

Chapter Fifty-four

Joseph ran over to the window to look out. "How are they coming?" he asked.

"Many of them are just walking, but some have cars," Cat replied. "Donovan said that he was able to take some of the back roads and get around them. But it will be close."

"We need to form a circle, now," Agnes said. "We need every advantage we can get."

"But Donovan's not here," Hazel reminded her. "And he's the strongest link."

"Why didn't he just transport himself here?" Rowan asked.

"I'm guessing it's because he's with Ellis," Henry said. "When we got here, Ellis took my car and headed back to the B&B to try and find the amulet too. He probably got there about the time Hazel arrived here."

"And he can't transport himself and Ellis," Cat agreed. "That makes sense."

332

"I can drive Ellis in," Hazel said. "Switch places with Donovan, so that you can do the circle."

Agnes paused. "We need you for the circle. Besides, they can't be too far away," she said with uncertainty.

Agnes turned to Cat. "Call Donovan and ask him where he is," she said. "Then tell him what we need to do."

Joseph moved back to the group. "I'm going up to the attic to get a bird's eye view of the situation," he said. "Then we'll be able to plan on how we can defend the house."

Cat called Donovan back. "We need you to be here," she said, "because of your connection to the amulet. And we need you here now."

"No problem," Donovan answered. "We're out in the country now, Ellis can drive the rest of the way without me. I'll be there in a moment."

It seemed to Cat that as soon as she disconnected the call, Donovan was standing in the kitchen.

"So, what do we need to do?" he asked.

She stared at him for a long moment. "You never told me that you could transport," she said.

He looked uncomfortable, and then he shrugged. "I guess it just never came up in our conversations."

"Donovan did you ever…" she began.

"Good! You're here," Agnes interrupted. "We need to get that circle going now."

Joseph ran down the steps. "We've got about ten minutes before the crowd gets here," he said. "There's some cars ahead of that."

He looked at Donovan. "You're not with Ellis?"

"No, he said that he could drive the rest of the way on his own," Donovan replied. "Did you see him?"

"Yeah, I saw Henry's car ahead of the covens," Joseph replied. "It looks like he'll be fine because the other cars seem to be waiting for the big crowd."

"Yeah, those covens are not made up of heroes, just sheep," Donovan said.

"Even sheep can be dangerous in a stampede," Joseph reminded him.

Donovan nodded. "You're right," he said. "Magic is not our only concern."

"Joseph and I will see what we can do to make some barriers, so it's not easy for them to get access to the house," Henry offered. "You five need to get that circle going now."

Joseph and Henry ran out the back door toward the barn. "I'm thinking straw bales across the driveway," Henry suggested.

"Good," Joseph agreed. "And let's move any big equipment out, to deter them too."

With a wave of his arms, Henry opened the large door to the barn loft. Then he turned to Joseph. "I can't even think straight, let alone create a rhyme. So, how do I get the bales down?" Henry asked.

Sighing, Joseph turned and looked up at the loft.

The barn is red,

The straw is brown,

Move those bales,

Down to the ground.

As soon as Joseph waved his arms, one by one, the large bales of straw slid to the edge of the opening and flew down across the barnyard to the driveway where they began to stack themselves up.

"Really? That was it?" Henry asked, amazed.

"Just let the words flow and don't think about it, it's magic, not brain surgery," Joseph replied with a grin. "Now, you might want to do something with Hazel's goats, so she's not worried about them."

Henry nodded and ran to the small pasture next to the barn. The back pasture wasn't any safer; the covens had already tried to kill some of her goats back in them, so he needed a place where they would be safely out of the way. He looked up to the nearly empty loft and smiled. "It could work," he said aloud.

He turned to the goats.

"To protect and disguise

All of Hazel's herd,

Up you all go,

Just like a bird."

The goats, bleating nervously, were lifted and levitated to the loft, high above the barn. One by one they soared, touching down gently on the wooden floor and then dashing toward the interior of the building. Once they were all safely inside, Henry waved his arms and closed and locked the loft doors so they couldn't fall out.

He turned, amazed at the sixteen-foot-high wall of straw, and nodded with satisfaction. They might be outnumbered, but they certainly weren't going to be out maneuvered.

Chapter Fifty-five

The rug was rolled away, and the Willoughbys were standing in place, with Donovan in the middle. The women at each corner of the quaternary knot cleared the circle with their smudge sticks and cleared the space in between.

With the area protected, Agnes turned to Rowan. "Do you have the spell?" she asked.

Rowan pulled out her phone and opened her photo application. "Yes, Henry sent me the picture he took of the page," she said, squinting at the old, cursive print. "Should I read it?"

Agnes nodded. "Yes, but read it as words, not as a spell."

"Okay," Rowan said, repeating the words Henry had read earlier.

We summon the sacred power of three,

To diminish the spell they created for thee,

The sisters will try, but will not succeed,

As I demand, so mote it be.

"So, we have to reverse it," Cat said. "Right?"

"We have to reverse some of it," Agnes said.
"And then redirect the magic."

"So, we dismiss the sacred power of three?" Hazel
asked.

Agnes shook her head. "No, I think we still need
that power to defeat him," she said thoughtfully.

"Why don't we redirect the sacred power of
three," Cat suggested.

"Oh, very good, dear," Agnes agreed. "We will
redirect the power, not dismiss it. What's next?"

"To diminish the spell they create for thee,"
Rowan read.

"How about to fulfill the spell they created for
thee?" Hazel asked.

"Perfect," Agnes agreed. "This is going much
faster than I thought." She turned to Rowan. "The next
line, dear."

"The sisters will try, but will not succeed," Rowan read.

"Well, these sisters are going to succeed," Cat said. "There is no other option."

"But the sisters aren't here anymore," Hazel added. "And if Donovan is a piece to this puzzle, it's not just about us anymore."

Cat looked up and met Donovan's eyes and saw the tender emotion in them. "How about love will overcome what hate decreed?" Donovan suggested softly, his gaze never leaving Cat's.

Agnes looked from Cat to Donovan and smiled. "Yes, that's it exactly," she said. "That's what we need."

She turned to Rowan. "Do you have the bowl with the amulet?" she asked.

Rowan slid the green earthen bowl into the middle of the circle next to Donovan.

"What am I supposed to do?" Donovan asked.

"We will recite the incantation," Rowan explained, "and we will concentrate our energies on you.

340

Then you need to concentrate all of that energy on the amulet, to melt it. Once it's melted, you need to stamp it with our quaternary knot, to give us access to the power."

He picked up the steel stamp that was next to him on the floor and looked at it. "The famous Willoughby knot," he said with a smile. "I'm honored to be able to use it."

The kitchen door flew open with a crash and, a moment later, Henry and Joseph rushed into the great room. "They're less than a mile down the road," Joseph said, his voice grim. "We don't have much time."

From within the protection of the circle, Agnes could hear the muted sound of Joseph's warning.

"We're almost ready," Agnes said. "All right girls, let's concentrate."

Each of the women raised their arms, so their fingers were nearly touching, and Agnes recited the spell.

We redirect the sacred power of three,

To fulfill the spell they create for thee,

Love will overcome what hate decreed,

341

As we request, so mote it be.

A blazing blue light shot from one woman to the next, until a circle was formed and then the light encompassed Donovan in the center. He felt the power filling him, healing him, as white magic pushed aside any darkness left inside. He inhaled sharply and then focused all of his energy onto the amulet. He watched a thin strand of smoke appear from the amulet, but it wasn't enough to melt it. He concentrated harder, focusing all he had on the small object in the bowl, but it just wouldn't melt.

Finally, the light ebbed, cooled, then dissipated completely and the circle's protection gave way

Chapter Fifty-six

The house shook as a bombardment of magic hit the roof.

"They're here," Agnes said, her voice shaking. "They're here, and we couldn't melt the amulet. I don't know what else we can do."

"I felt it," Donovan said. "I felt the power inside me, but there was something missing." Then he looked at Cat. "No, there was someone missing."

"What?" Cat asked, shaking her head. "I don't understand."

"This spell is about love overcoming hate," he said. "But it's also about love overcoming fear. I was afraid Cat. I was afraid that I wasn't good enough for you to love. I was afraid that I was just one of your strays." He shook his head and lowered his voice. "I was afraid that you would eventually stop loving me."

She moved from her position in the knot and took his hands. "You never left me, did you?" she asked, gazing up into his eyes. "You came to me, comforted me in my sleep."

He leaned over and kissed her softly. "I couldn't help myself," he confessed. "I couldn't stay away from you. I love you, Cat."

"I love you too," she replied, returning his kiss.

Another volley of magic hit the house, causing the walls to shake.

"We have to be in the center together," Donovan said. "The magic has to come through both of us. It has to be created by both of us."

Cat nodded. "Yes. That's the solution," she agreed. "We have to do this together."

Agnes shook her head. "But we need someone at each of the corners of the knot," she said frantically. "Someone related by blood. How can we..."

"Will I do?" Finias asked, stepping forward.

Agnes' eyes widened in shock, her hand lifting as she covered her mouth in surprise. "Finias?" she sobbed quietly.

He knelt next to her and took her hands. "It's time, Agnes," he said.

"Wait, this is Ellis," Hazel said. "Not Finias."

Agnes shook her head, her eyes glued on the man next to her. "No, this is Finias," she whispered. "My first love. Cat's father."

"Okay, I didn't see that coming," Joseph said. "But if Finias can stand in for Cat, I suggest you do this right away. Henry and I can hold them off for a little while, but we're going to need the cavalry soon!"

Agnes inhaled her tears and nodded. "Yes, we can do this," she said, her voice shaking. "We can do this now."

Finias stepped into the circle where Cat had been sitting. "I don't think we have time to cleanse again," he said.

Agnes nodded. "It's not necessary," she said, her voice stronger as the magic filled her. "The magic of the circle still surrounds us."

Donovan wrapped Cat in his arms, and she placed her head on his shoulder.

"I'll love you forever, Catalpa Willoughby," he whispered into her ear.

She smiled, and her eyes filled with tears. "I'll love you even longer," she whispered back.

Then Agnes repeated the spell.

We redirect the sacred power of three,

To fulfill the spell they create for thee,

Love will overcome what hate decreed,

As we request, so mote it be.

Blue light turned to molten gold as it encircled the group and then spilled over the couple in the center of the circle. With hands clenched together, Cat and Donovan turned their energy to the earthen pot and the amulet dissolved into a pool of liquid. Cat picked up the Willoughby crest and pressed it against the hot lead, emblazing its imprint on the amulet.

Chapter Fifty-seven

When Cat lifted her hand away, a golden burst of magic shot out from the center of the earthen pot and up, flowing over the outside of the protective circle. The sound was like being underneath a powerful waterfall as wave after wave of magic pulsed up and over.

It spread, like a wave across the room, knocking over furniture, and pushing open doors, flowing outside. Cat and Donovan held each other tightly in the center of the circle, and the other members clasped hands as the energy flowed through them and out.

Joseph ran into the house, his face alight with excitement. "Whatever the hell you're doing, keep it up," he called, and he ran back outside.

Henry, his arms wrapped around the porch post to keep from being dragged away, called out to Joseph. "What's going on?"

Joseph, carefully making his way to the post across from Henry, shook his head and shouted over the roar of the magic. "I guess they got the amulet spell to work."

Henry looked out over the farmyard. Hundreds of men and women dressed in black cloaks were making their way forward. Many were carrying knives and swords, and in front of the group, the serpent swirled and hissed. It's forked tongue tasting the fear in the air.

Henry watched as some ran ahead, charging across the lawn and approaching the fence line. Others had started climbing up the bales of straw and had nearly climbed over the tops, their weapons in their hands. Others were moving toward the front of the house. But the wave of magic seemed to be slowing them down.

Fuzzy stood next to them, growling deep in his throat, quivering and waiting for the command to attack.

"Easy Fuzzy," Joseph said. "We're not ready to charge until we see the whites of their eyes."

"The magic from the amulet is getting in the way, but we're going to need their help if this group gets any closer," Henry called.

Joseph ran back into the house. "The magic is helping," he called. "But they're still getting closer. Can you do anything more?"

"Concentrate," Cat said. "Concentrate on the power of love."

She turned to Donovan, her eyes filled with emotion. "The long-lasting power of love."

He bent over and kissed her. Then, suddenly, like a tsunami wave, the magic pulled back, allowing the intruders to move forward quickly.

"Whatever you did," Joseph called from the kitchen door, watching the intruders get closer. "Don't do it again."

Donovan broke off the kiss. "Concentrate on the people you love," he said. "Use that emotion to protect and overcome evil."

All eyes closed, as each member of the group pictured the one they held closest in their hearts. Donovan pulled Cat closer. "I will never leave you," he said. "Never again."

She looked up into his eyes and smiled. "I trust you, Donovan," she whispered. "I trust you with my love and my heart."

Joseph ran back outside to stand next to Henry as the intruders entered the farmyard. "What are the odds?" he asked.

Henry smiled and shrugged. "Well, if you believe that good conquers evil, the odds are in our favor."

Joseph nodded, positioning himself in a defensive stance. "Of course, I believe," he said. "Ready to fight?"

Henry nodded. "Always!"

Henry and Joseph started climbing down the stairs, ready to fight when they were knocked to the side by a burst of golden energy. They grabbed the handrails as the magic burst forward with even more power. It flowed through the farmyard, carrying with it the intruders that had breached the fences and the bales. It knocked over the bales of straw, trapping people underneath. It knocked over the fences, like a tornado, pulling the fence posts up out of the ground, sending intruders flying backwards onto the road. It rolled forward, its rolling power catching people up and pushing them backwards.

The giant serpent lifted itself to its full height and hissed at the approaching golden cloud of magic. Its form started to change from physical to mystical, a dark, black cloud swirling in the center of the road.

Joseph and Henry pulled themselves up onto the porch and watched as the golden wave approached the dark, swirling mass.

"We should give it a hand," Henry said, focusing his magical energy on the wave.

"Right there with you," Joseph agreed, concentrating with all his might.

The two forces swirled around each other, like two tornados. Pieces of earth whipped across the sky, power poles were uprooted and flung into nearby fields, the Willoughby house shook from the force of the energy.

As Joseph and Henry watched, they couldn't tell which force was greater. Black and gold swirled together for what seemed like hours, but was, in actuality only minutes. Finally, the darkness slowly dissipated, like the sun coming out from behind the clouds. The golden wave pushed forward, knocking back any of the remaining intruders who were now running away because their leader had vanished before their eyes.

Henry leaned back against the porch pillar and wiped the sweat from his forehead. He looked across at Joseph, who was doing the same thing, and smiled. "I love a happy ending," he gasped.

Joseph grinned. "Me too."

Chapter Fifty-eight

The magic stilled inside the circle, the gold light turned to blue, and then slowly faded away.

"Is it over?" Cat asked, her voice shaking. "Did we win?"

Donovan stood up and helped her to her feet. "There's only one way to find out," he said, slipping his arm around her and leading outside.

The sun was shining down on the countryside, but the area looked like a bomb has exploded.

"What happened?" Agnes asked, as she stepped outside, Finias at her side.

"I think it was you," Joseph said, coming over and kissing Hazel. "Yes, when I write up my police report, I'm going to totally blame it on you."

Hazel smiled up at him. "I can't wait to read that report," she teased.

Henry walked over to Rowan and kissed her soundly. "Sorry I missed the excitement inside," he said.

She shook her head and looked at the devastation. "It looks like there was enough excitement outside to keep you busy," she exclaimed. "Did you take any prisoners?"

He shook his head. "No, I think they are all retreating right now."

"Really?" Hazel asked. "I'm going to get a better view."

She immediately disappeared, only to suddenly reappear as she pushed open the loft's door. She gazed down the road and laughed gleefully. "They're running," she called down to the others. "They're running in the opposite direction. We kicked butt! We kicked magic butt!"

Then she shouted again as she was pushed from behind. "Hey, what's going on?"

She turned back to the loft and then looked back down at her family on the deck. "Who thought putting my goats in the loft was a good idea?" she yelled down.

Henry shrugged and wrapped his arm around Rowan. "Seemed like a good idea at the time."

Hazel reappeared next to them and looked at Henry. "And you get to help me clean up the mess," she ordered.

He smiled at her. "Yes, ma'am," he agreed. "But first we need a celebration. Right, Agnes…"

He turned and saw that Agnes and Finias were at the far end of the deck, absorbed in their own conversation. He shook his head and smiled at Rowan. "I guess they probably want to be left alone," he suggested. "We should all probably…"

He looked the other way and saw Cat and Donovan locked in each other's arms at the other end of the deck. "Okay, well maybe the four of us just ought to go inside," he said.

Rowan chuckled and nodded. "I think that's a great idea."

"How about take out?" Hazel suggested. "I know a great place."

Chapter Fifty-nine

Donovan and Cat walked up the trail, hand in hand, the moonlight illuminating their way. The cool, early autumn breeze rustled the leaves around them, and the wind carried the scent of a distant campfire. Cat sighed, her voice slightly shaking, and Donovan turned to her.

"Are you cold?" he asked, concerned.

She smiled up at him and shook her head. "No, I was just thinking about tonight. How close we all came..." she paused, and her voice shook as she glanced around. "Are you sure we're safe?"

He leaned down and pressed a gentle kiss on her lips. "Yes, we're safe," he said softly. "I brought this with us, just in case."

He reached into his jeans pocket and pulled out the newly formed amulet with the Willoughby crest emblazoned into it. "It's now my good luck charm," he said.

"Good luck?" she asked skeptically. "It doesn't seem like a good luck charm to me."

"Sure, it is," he said with a smile. "It brought us back together, didn't it?"

She shook her head. "No, it didn't bring us back together," she insisted. "But it did remind us of what we have."

He sighed, wrapped his arms around her, and leaned his forehead against hers. "I'm so sorry for all the pain I caused you," he whispered. "I should have trusted you more. I should have trusted us more."

She slipped her arms around his waist. "You weren't the only one with doubts and fears," she confessed.

He leaned back and looked into her eyes. "I want you to know that I have never stopped loving you," he said. "Not for one moment. Even when the demon was influencing me, there was always a part of me that still loved you, still wanted to protect you."

She trembled as she thought about the influence the demon had had on him. "Promise me," she said vehemently, "that you will never allow the demon to influence you again, even if you think it's to protect me."

He nodded. "I was stupid to think that I could dabble in the darkness and not get caught up," he said. "From now on, we fight this thing together, and we do it from the side of light, I promise."

"Thank you," she replied, reminding herself that she needed to be content with whatever he was willing to offer. Fighting together, saving her family, those were priceless gifts. Loving her didn't necessarily mean that he wanted to be with her forever.

He studied her eyes. "There's still sadness in your eyes, Cat," he said, tenderly stroking her cheek. "Why are you sad?"

She shook her head and blinked away the tears his tenderness had caused. "It's nothing," she said. "I'm just grateful that you are safe and we're both on the same side.

I'm grateful to you for saving my family. And I'm grateful for what we've been able to share."

He studied her for a long moment but said nothing, just took her hand and led her further up the trail, to the cave they'd hidden in so many years ago.

"Why are you bringing me here?" she asked.

He smiled at her, but his eyes were mysterious. "I think there's a storm approaching," he said.

"No," she replied, looking up to the night sky. "There's not a cloud for…"

Tiny, shimmering drops of rain suddenly fell on her face, and she turned to him in surprise. He laughed and pulled her into the cave. "You need to get out of the rain, Catalpa," he said, his voice thick and low as he guided her into his arms.

The rain increased, creating a curtain between them and the outside world. He leaned forward, kissed the side of her neck, and then trailed light kisses along her jawbone. She sighed softly.

"So sweet," he murmured, kissing her cheeks and her forehead. "So, incredibly sweet."

His hands slid up her rain-slickened arms and then slid onto her back, pulling her even closer, molding her to him. Then he lowered his mouth and teased her lips, sliding over them, tenderly kissing them until she sighed and moaned, giving him full access to her sweetness.

He crushed his lips against hers, tasting, teasing, and exploring. She trembled again, her body shaking with reaction.

"Donovan," she breathed.

His name on her lips flamed the fire of his passion, and he deepened the kiss. Nothing existed, but the two of them in their own secluded world.

He felt her body lean against his for support. Felt the pounding of her heart against his chest. But when he reached inside her mind to make the most intimate of connections, he sensed fear.

He slowly pulled away, kissing her lightly as he helped her stand on her own. She looked up at him, her lips swollen from his kisses, her face flush with passion, and her eyes filled with love and confusion.

"Donovan?" she questioned as she returned his gaze. "What?"

"I should have realized," he said regretfully, leaning in to kiss her gently on her forehead. "I remembered this place as the place where I met the most beautiful girl in the world." Then he shook his head. "But you remember it as the place I said good-bye to you."

A single tear rolled down her cheek, and she tried to shrug casually. "We were children," she whispered, her voice raw. "We didn't know…"

He gently placed his finger over her lips to stop her. "We knew," he said. "I knew that you were my one true love. I knew that I needed to prove myself – not just to you, but to myself too." He slowly slid his finger from her lips and placed a kiss there instead. "But I also knew that someday I would come back and ask you a question."

Still confused and wary, Cat shook her head. "What question?" she stammered.

361

Kneeling before her on one knee, he took her hands in his. Suddenly, the cave was illuminated with a thousand tiny lights, and sweet music was echoing in the small chamber.

Donovan lifted his hand, then opened it to reveal a sparkling diamond ring and Catalpa's heart soared. "Catalpa Willoughby, will you do me the great honor of becoming my wife?"

With tears in her eyes, she nodded her head. "Oh, yes," she whispered. "Oh, yes, I will."

He stood up, wrapped his arms around her, and kissed her with all the love he possessed. "I always have and will always love you," he vowed.

She lifted her hand and rested it against his cheek, her eyes were blazing with love and joy, and her heart was overflowing with happiness. "And I always have and will always love you," she replied. "You are and have always been my knight in shining armor."

Chapter Sixty

Back at the Willoughy house, Hazel leaned over the table and looked at Finias. "So, why did you tell us your name was Ellis?" she asked. "Are you running from the law or something?"

Finias laughed and shook his head. "No, but I had agreed a long time ago that I would not interfere with the Willoughby spell," he said. "But I had a premonition that things were not going to go as smoothly as planned, so I decided to come here and assume another identity."

"Good premonition," Hazel said, grabbing another piece of pizza and sitting back in her chair. "Really good premonition."

"So, you've been Cat's spirit guide since she was little, right?" Henry asked.

Finias nodded. "Perhaps I stretched the rules," he said. "But I could not keep myself from being a part of my daughter's life."

Agnes took his hand in hers and smiled up at him. "And, if you study the spirit of the law, he wasn't interfering with the spell by being Cat's guide."

"Yeah, but a dad being a guide," Hazel said, "was it hard not just to tell her what to do?"

"Cat was always a reasonable young woman," Finias countered, hiding a smile.

Rowan nodded. "She had to be because Mom was so crazy," Rowan teased.

Finias lifted their joined hands and placed a kiss on Agnes' palm. "That's one of the things I fell in love with," he said softly, his eyes locked with hers.

"Did your premonition tell you anything that we can use for Samhain?" Joseph asked.

Finias shook his head slowly. "Well, as you know, when you have visions that either includes yourself or people you love, they can often be unclear or incomplete," he said. "I do know that there was something about danger, something about a hidden secret, and then something about a long journey."

"One of us is going to take a long journey?" Hazel asked. "That doesn't seem likely."

"No," Finias said thoughtfully. "It seemed more like someone was going to journey here."

"To help us or to hurt us?" Henry asked.

Finias shrugged. "That was unclear."

"I can see why you came," Joseph said. "There seems to be uncertainty and danger in the road ahead."

Rowan sighed. "Well, I suppose we'll find out soon enough," she said. "Samhain is only five weeks away."

A lull fell over the conversation as each person at the table felt the weight of Rowan's words. Hazel placed her hands over her belly, and Joseph turned to her, placing his hands over hers. "I promise you," he whispered to her. "That I will protect you and our child."

She looked up at him, her eyes glittering with unshed tears, and nodded. "I'm afraid," she whispered back. "It's so close, and I'm afraid."

Suddenly, the peal of the doorbell made them all jump.

"Stay still," Joseph commanded, jumping up and reaching for his service revolver. "I'll get it."

But they all got up and followed him to the front door.

"Stop!" Agnes commanded as the men started to take defensive positions around the door. They all looked back at her in surprise. "This is my house, and I will answer the door."

She marched past them, opened the door, and gasped aloud.

"What?" Hazel and Rowan shouted, hurrying to their mother's side.

They stopped on either side of her and stared at the two men that stood on the front porch.

Agnes took a deep breath and then sighed. "Rowan, Hazel," she finally said. "I'd like to introduce you to your fathers."

The End

About the author: Terri Reid lives near Freeport, the home of the Mary O'Reilly Mystery Series, and loves a good ghost story. An independent author, Reid uploaded her first book "Loose Ends – A Mary O'Reilly Paranormal Mystery" in August 2010. By the end of 2013, "Loose Ends" had sold over 200,000 copies. She has sixteen other books in the Mary O'Reilly Series, the first books in the following series - "The Blackwood Files," "The Order of Brigid's Cross," and "The Legend of the Horsemen." She also has a stand-alone romance, "Bearly in Love." Reid has enjoyed Top Rated and Hot New Release status in the Women Sleuths and Paranormal Romance category through Amazon US. Her books have been translated into Spanish, Portuguese and German and are also now also available in print and audio versions. Reid has been quoted in several books about the self-publishing industry including "Let's Get Digital" by David Gaughran and "Interviews with Indie Authors: Top Tips from Successful Self-Published Authors" by Claire and Tim Ridgway. She was also honored to have some of

368

her works included in A. J. Abbiati's book "The

NORTAV Method for Writers – The Secrets to

Constructing Prose Like the Pros."

She loves hearing from her readers at

author@terrireid.com

Other Books by Terri Reid:

Mary O'Reilly Paranormal Mystery Series:

Loose Ends (Book One)

Good Tidings (Book Two)

Never Forgotten (Book Three)

Final Call (Book Four)

Darkness Exposed (Book Five)

Natural Reaction (Book Six)

Secret Hollows (Book Seven)

Broken Promises (Book Eight)

Twisted Paths (Book Nine)

Veiled Passages (Book Ten)

Bumpy Roads (Book Eleven)

Treasured Legacies (Book Twelve)

Buried Innocence (Book Thirteen)

Stolen Dreams (Book Fourteen)

Haunted Tales (Book Fifteen)

Deadly Circumstances (Book Sixteen)

Frayed Edges (Book Seventeen)

Delayed Departures (Book Eighteen)

Old Acquaintance (Book Nineteen)

Clear Expectations (Book Twenty)

Finders Mansion Mystery Series

Maybelle's Secret

Maybelle's Affair

Mary O'Reilly Short Stories

The Three Wise Guides

Tales Around the Jack O'Lantern 1

Tales Around the Jack O'Lantern 2

Tales Around the Jack O'Lantern 3

Auld Lang Syne

The Order of Brigid's Cross (Sean's Story)

The Wild Hunt (Book 1)

The Faery Portal (Book 2)

The Blackwood Files (Art's Story)

File One: Family Secrets

File Two: Private Wars

Eochaidh: Legend of the Horseman (Book One)

Eochaidh: Legend of the Horsemen (Book Two)

Sweet Romances

Bearly in Love

Sneakers – A Swift Romance

Lethal Distraction – A Pierogies & Pumps Mystery Novella

The Willoughby Witches

Rowan's Responsibility

Hazel's Heart

Made in the USA
Monee, IL
15 August 2021